The Seamstress and the Wind

ALSO BY CÉSAR AIRA FROM NEW DIRECTIONS

An Episode in the Life of a Landscape Painter

Ghosts

How I Became a Nun

The Literary Conference

The Seamstress and the Wind

•

CÉSAR AIRA

Translated by Rosalie Knecht

A NEW DIRECTIONS PAPERBOOK ORIGINAL

Originally published by Beatriz Viterbo Editoria, Rosario, Argentina, as *La costurera y el viento* in 1994; published in conjunction with the literary agency Michael Gaeb / Berlin

Manufactured in the United States of America
New Directions Books are printed on acid-free paper.
First published as a New Directions Paperbook Original (NDP1203) in 2011
Published simultaneously in Canada by Penguin Books Canada Limited
Design by Erik Rieselbach

Library of Congress Cataloging-in-Publication Data
Aira, César, 1949–
[Costurera y el viento. English]
The seamstress and the wind / César Aira ; translated from the Spanish by Rosalie Knecht.
p. cm.
Originally published by in Argentina as La costurera y el viento, in 1994.
ISBN-13: 978-0-8112-1912-9 (paperbook : alk. paper)
ISBN-10: 0-8112-1912-7 (pbk. : alk. paper)
1. Women dressmakers—Argentina—Fiction. 2. Patagonia (Argentina and Chile)—Fiction. I. Knecht, Rosalie. II. Title.
PQ7798.1.I7C6713 2011
863'.64—dc22

2011006006

10 9 8 7 6 5 4 3 2

New Directions Books are published for James Laughlin
by New Directions Publishing Corporation
80 Eighth Avenue, New York, NY 10011

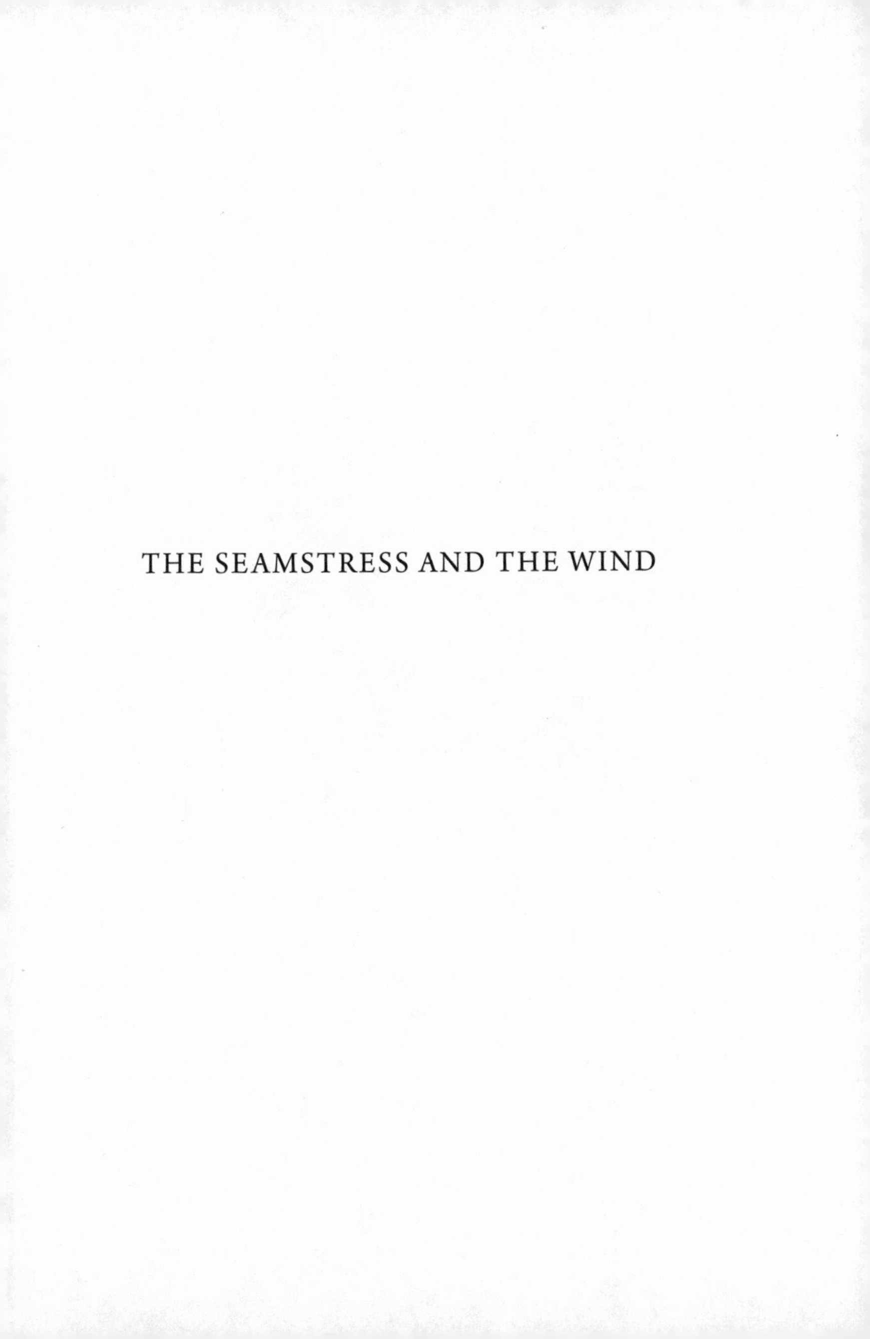

THE SEAMSTRESS AND THE WIND

1

THESE LAST WEEKS, since before coming to Paris, I've been looking for a plot for the novel I want to write: a novel of successive adventures, full of anomalies and inventions. Until now nothing occurred to me, except the title, which I've had for years and which I cling to with blank obstinacy: "The Seamstress and the Wind." The heroine has to be a seamstress, at a time when there were seamstresses . . . and the wind her antagonist, she sedentary, he a traveler, or the other way around: the art a traveler, the turbulence fixed. She the adventure, he the thread of the adventures . . . It could be anything, and in fact it must be anything, any whim, or all of them, if they begin transforming into one another . . . For once I want to allow myself every liberty, even the most improbable . . . Although the most improbable, I should admit, is that this plan will work. The gusts of the imagination do not carry one away except when one has not asked for it, or better: when one has asked for the opposite. And then there is the question of finding a good plot.

Anyway, last night, this morning, at dawn, still half asleep, or more asleep than I thought I was, a subject occurred to me—rich, complex, unexpected. Not all of it, just the beginning, but that was just what I needed, what I had been waiting for. The character was a man, which wasn't a problem because I could make him the seamstress's husband... However, when I woke up I had forgotten it. I only remembered that I had had it, and it was good, and now I didn't have it. In those cases it's not worth the trouble to wrack your brain, I know from experience, because nothing comes back, maybe because there is nothing, there never was anything, except the perfectly gratuitous sensation that there had been something... Still, the sensation is not complete; a vague little trace remains, in which I hope there is a loose end that I could pull and pull... although then, to go on with the metaphor, pulling on that strand would erase the embroidered figure and I would be left with a meaningless white thread between my fingers. It's about... let me see if I can put it in a few sentences: A man has a very precise and detailed premonition of three or four events that will happen in the immediate future all linked together. Not events which will happen to him, but to three or four neighbors, out in the country. He enters a state of accelerated movement to make use of his information: speed is necessary because the efficacy of the trick is in arriving on time, at the point at which the events coincide... He runs from one house to another like a billiard ball bouncing on the pampas... I get this far. I see nothing more. Actually, the thing I see least is the novelistic merit of this subject.

I'm sure in the dream all that senseless agitation came wrapped in a precise and admirable mechanism, but now I don't know what that was. The key to the code has been erased. Or is that what I should provide myself, with my deliberate work? If so, the dream doesn't have the least use, and it leaves me as unequipped as before, or more so. But I resist giving it up, and in that resistance it occurs to me that there's something else I could rescue from the ruins of forgetting, and that is forgetting itself. Taking control of forgetting is little more than a gesture, but it would be a gesture consistent with my theory of literature, at least with my disdain for memory as a writer's instrument. Forgetting is richer, freer, more powerful . . . and at the root of the dream idea there must have been something of that, because those serial prophecies, so suspicious, lacking in content as they are, all seem to come to an end at a vertex of dissolution, of forgetting, of pure reality. A multiple, impersonal forgetting. I should note, in parentheses, that the kind of forgetting that erases dreams is very special, and very fitting for my purposes, because it's based on doubt as to whether the thing we should be remembering actually exists; I suppose that in the majority of cases, if not in all of them, we only believe we've forgotten things when actually they had never happened. We haven't forgotten anything. Forgetting is simply a sensation.

2

FORGETTING BECOMES SIMPLY a sensation. It drops the object, as in a disappearance. It's our whole life, that object of the past, that falls into the antigravity updrafts of adventure.

There's been little adventure. None, in fact. I don't remember any. And I don't think it's by chance, like when you stop to think and realize that in the whole past year you haven't seen a single dwarf. My life must be shaped around that lack of adventure, which is lamentable because it would have been a good source of inspiration. But I've sought out that lack of adventure myself, and in the future I will do it on purpose. A few days ago, before I left, reflecting, I came to the conclusion that I will never travel again. I won't go out looking for adventure. To tell the truth, I've never traveled. This trip, the same as the previous one (when I wrote *El Llanto*), can only come to nothing, a spiral of the imagination. If I now write, in the cafés of Paris, *The Seamstress and the Wind,* as I have proposed, it's only to accelerate the process. What process? A process with no name, or form, or content. Or results. If it helps me survive, it's only the way some little riddle would have. I think that for a process to be sustained over time there must always be the intrigue of a point out of place. But nothing will be discovered in the end, or at the beginning either, because the decision has already been made: I will never travel again. Suddenly, I'm in a café in Paris, writing, giving expression to anachronistic decisions made in the very heart of the fear of adventure (in a café in my neighborhood, Flores). A person can come to believe he has another life, in addition to his own, and logically he believes that he has it somewhere else, waiting for him. But you only have to test this theory once to see it doesn't hold. One trip is enough (I made two). There's only one life, and it is in its place. But still, something must have happened. If I've written, it's been so I might interpolate forgetfulness between my life and myself. I was successful there. When a memory appears, it brings nothing with it, only a combination of itself and its negative aftereffects. And the whirlwind. And me. In some ways the "Seamstress and the Wind" have to do with (and are the most appropriate to, and even, I would almost say, the only fitting thing for) a strange quotation. I would prefer them to be the pure invention of my soul, now that my soul has been extracted from me. But they still aren't, after all, nor could they be, because reality, or the past, contaminates them. I raise barriers, hoping they're formidable, to impede the invasion, though I know the battle is already lost. I didn't have an adventurous life because I didn't want to weigh myself down with memories ... "Perhaps it is an exclusively personal point of view, but I experience an irrepressible distrust when I hear it said that the imagination will take care of everything.

"The imagination, this marvelous faculty, does nothing, if left uncontrolled, but lean on memory.

"Memory makes things felt, heard and seen rise into the light, a bit the way a bolus of grass rises again in a ruminant. It may be chewed, but it is neither digested nor transformed." (Boulez)

3

IT'S NOT RANDOM, I said. I have a biographical motive to back up this reasoning. My first experience, the first of those events that leave a mark, was a disappearance. I would have been eight or nine. I was playing in the street with my friend Omar, and it occurred to us to climb into the empty trailer of a truck parked in front of our houses (we were neighbors). The trailer was an enormous rectangle, the size of a room, that had three high wooden walls without a fourth, which was the back. It was perfectly empty and clean. We began to play at scaring each other, which is strange because it was in the middle of the day, we had no masks or disguises or anything else, and that space, of all those we could have picked, was the most geometric and visible. It was a purely psychological game of fantasy. I don't know how such subtlety could have occurred to us, a couple of semi-savage children, but kids are like that. And the fear turned out to be more effective than we expected. On the first try, it was already excessive. Omar began. I sat on the floor, close to the back edge, and he went and stood by the front wall. He said "Now" and started walking toward me with heavy, slow steps, without making faces or gestures (it wasn't necessary) ... I felt such terror that I must have closed my eyes ... When I opened them, Omar wasn't there. I was paralyzed, strangled, as in a nightmare; I wanted to move but couldn't. It was as if a wind were pressing in on me from all sides at once. I felt deformed, twisted, both ears on the same side of my head, both eyes on the other, an arm coming out of my navel, the other from my back, the left foot coming out of the right thigh ... Squatting, like an octidimensional toad ... I had the impression, which I knew so well, of running desperately to escape a danger, a horror ... to escape the crouching monster that I now was. All I could do was stay in the safest place.

All at once, I don't know how, I found myself in the kitchen of my house, behind the table. My mother was standing at the counter with her back to me, looking out the window. She was not working, not making food or tidying things, which was very strange for a classic housewife who was always doing something; but her immobility was full of impatience. I knew because I had a telepathic connection with her. And she with me: she must have felt my presence, because she turned abruptly and saw me. She let out a yell like I've never heard from her and brought both hands to her head with a moan of anguish, almost a sob, something she'd never done before but which I knew was within her expressive capabilities. It was as if something impossible had happened, something unimaginable. By the shouting she subjected me to when she was able to articulate again I found out that Omar had come, at noon, to say I'd hidden and wouldn't reappear despite his calling me and his declarations that he wasn't playing anymore, that he had to go. Such obstinacy was typical of me, but as the hours passed they started to get alarmed, mamá joined the search, and in the end papá intervened (this was the highest degree of alarm) and was still looking for me, with the help of Omar's father and I don't know which other neighbors, in a by-the-book search party through the immediate area, and she hadn't been able to do anything, she hadn't started making dinner, she hadn't even had the heart to turn on the lights ... I saw that, in fact, it was already very dark out—it was almost night. But I had been there the whole time! I didn't say this to her because I was too emotional to speak. It wasn't me, they were wrong ... it was Omar who'd disappeared! It was his mother who had to be told, a search for him that had to be undertaken. And now, I thought in a spasm of desperation, it would be much more difficult because night was falling. I felt responsible for the lost time, whose irretrievable quality I understood for the first time.

4

IT'S INCREDIBLE, THE speed a chain of events can take, starting with one that could be called immobile. It's a kind of vertigo; straightaway events do not occur: they become simultaneous. It's the ideal resource for getting rid of memory, for making an anachronism of any recollection. Starting from that slip of mine, everything began to happen at once. Especially for Delia Siffoni, Omar's mother. Her son's disappearance affected her deeply, it affected her mind, which must have surprised me since she wasn't the emotional type; she was one of those women, so abundant then in Pringles, on the poor outskirts where we lived, who—before ceasing to bear children forever—had a single child, a boy, and raised him with a certain severe coolness. Each of my friends was an only child, each more or less the same age, each with that kind of mother. They were maniacal about cleanliness, they did not allow dogs, they acted like widows. And always:

a single male child. I don't know how, later on, there came to be women in Argentina.

Delia Siffoni and my mother had been friends when they were children. Then she'd left town, and when she came back, married and with a six- or seven-year-old boy, she ended up renting, completely by chance, the house next to ours. The two friends were reacquainted. And the two of us, Omar and I, became inseparable, all day together in the street. Our mothers, on the other hand, maintained that distance tinged with malevolence typical of the local women. Mamá found many defects in Delia, but that was practically a hobby for her. In the first place, she thought Delia was crazy, unbalanced: they all were, when you started thinking about it. Then the mania for cleaning; you have to recognize that Delia was exemplary. She kept her little parlor hermetically sealed, and no one ever entered it under any pretext. The single bedroom was resplendent, and so was the kitchen. Those three rooms were the whole house, and their house was an exact copy of ours. Several times a day she swept both patios, the front and the back, including the chicken coop; and the sidewalk, which was dirt, was always sprayed down. She devoted herself to that. We'd nicknamed her "the pigeon," because of her nose and eyes; my mother was an expert at finding animal resemblances. The way Delia talked also contributed to this: her voice was whispery and abrupt, as were her manners and movements when she was on the sidewalk (she was always outside: another defect): she would move away from her interlocutor with light little steps and then come back again, a thousand times, she'd go, she'd come back, she'd remember something else she had to say . . .

Delia had a profession, a trade, which made her an exception among the women of the neighborhood, who were only housewives and mothers, like mine. She was a seamstress (a seamstress, exactly, now I see the coincidence); she could even have made a living with her work, and in fact she did, because her husband had I don't know what vague shipping job and you couldn't really say that he worked in the broadest terms. She had a good reputation as a seamstress, trustworthy and very neat, although she had terrible taste. She did everything perfectly, but you had to give her very precise instructions and keep an eye on her up to the very last minute or she would ruin it by following some nefarious inspiration. But fast, she was extremely fast. When the customers came for a fitting ... There were four fittings, that was canonic in Pringlense couture. With Delia, the four fittings were muddled together in an instant, and anyway the garment was already finished. With her there was no time to change your mind, or anything else. She had lost a lot of her clientele because of it. She was always losing customers; it was a miracle she had any left. New ones were always appearing, that was the thing. Her supernatural velocity attracted them, like moths to a candle.

5

IN THE SUMMER, birds woke me. We had only one bedroom for the whole family, in the front of the house, facing the street. My bed was under the window. My parents, country people, were in the habit of sleeping with the window closed; but I had read in the *Billiken* children's magazine that it was much healthier to have it open, so when everyone was asleep I would stand on my bed and open it, barely a centimeter, without making the tiniest noise. The uproar of the little birds in the trees out front reached me before anyone else. I was the first one awake, startled by that burst of sharp sounds, just as I had been the last to fall asleep, at the end of an interminable session of mental horrors. And yet it always turned out that my mother had fallen asleep after me, and woken up before. I would find out indirectly, by some remark, and later I knew she stayed up past midnight knitting, sewing, listening to the radio, playing the piano—that last one was a curious pastime, but she had once been the town pianist, she had neither time nor desire to practice in the daytime, and it never woke me up. When the birds did wake me in the morning she had already been bustling around for some time. I don't know how that could have been, because without denying one reality, I went on believing the other: that I lay awake while she slept, that I even saw her sleeping (I believe I see her still), sleeping profoundly, abandoned to sleep, which made her more beautiful. Her wakefulness was misfiled in sleep. Might she have been a sleepwalker? Her curious habit of playing the piano (Clementi, Mozart, Chopin, Beethoven, and a transcription of *Lucia di Lammermoor*) in the depths of the night suggested it. I never heard it, she must have made sure I was sound asleep, but to this day I can evoke that supernaturally sedative nocturnal music, each note untying every knot in my life. That must be where my tortured passion for music started, music I don't understand, the strangest, most absurd, most avant-garde—to me none of it seems advanced or incomprehensible enough. As an adult, I discovered that my mother slept deeply, she was privileged, a Queen of Sleep, one of those people who could sleep forever, all their lives, if they set themselves to it. But back then she had the coquetry of insomnia, and when by chance she referred to the night it was to say "I didn't sleep a wink." Like all children, I must have believed her word for word. I am also a King of Sleep; I sleep like a log.

In the summer I woke up very early, with the birds, because the dawn was very early then, much earlier than now. Time didn't change according to the seasons then, and Pringles was very far south, where the days were longer. At four, I think, the chorus of birds would begin. But there was one, one bird, the one that woke me up on those summer mornings, a bird with the strangest and most beautiful song you could imagine. I never heard anything like it afterwards. His twittering was atonal, insanely modern, a melody of random notes, sharp, clean, crystalline. It was special because it was so unexpected, as if a scale existed and the bird chose four or five notes from it in an order that systematically sidestepped any expectations. But the order could not *always* be unexpected, there is no method like that: by pure chance it would have to meet some expectation, the law of probabilities demands it. And yet, it did not.

In fact, it was not a bird. It was Mr. Siffoni's truck, when he turned the crank. In those days you had to turn a crank on the front of a car to make the engine turn over. This was a really old vehicle, a little square truck, a red tin can, and it wasn't clear how it kept running. After the marvelous trill came the pathetic coughing of the engine. I wonder if that wasn't what woke me up, and that I imagined the previous. I often have, even today, these waking dreams. That one gave them the model.

The little red truck stood out against the clean and beautiful colors of the Pringlense dawn, the perfect blue sky, the green trees, the golden dirt of our street. The summer was the only season when Ramón Siffoni worked as a trucker. He relaxed the rest of the year. Not even in season did he work much, according to my parents, who criticized him for it. He didn't even get up early, they said (but I knew the truth).

Next to our house on the other side lived a professional trucker, a real one. He had a very modern truck, enormous, with a trailer (the very same one in which Omar and I had played on that ill-fated day), and he made long trips to the most distant reaches of Argentina. Not just in summer, like Siffoni making casual fair-weather hauls in his toy truck, but serious trips. His name was Chiquito, he was half-related to us, and sometimes when I left for school in the dead of winter, when the sky was still dark, I would find that he'd left me a snowman on the doorstep, a sign that he'd gone off on a long trip.

The snowman ... the lovely postcard of the little red truck in the pale blue and green dawn ... the senses celebrating. And all of that was suddenly shaken by the disappearance.

6

MY PARENTS WERE realistic people, enemies of fantasy. They judged everything by work, their universal standard for measuring their fellow man. Everything else hung on that criterion, which I inherited wholly and without question; I have always venerated work above all else; work is my god and my universal judge, but I never worked, because I never needed to, and my passion exempted me from working because of a bad conscience or a fear of what others might say.

In family conversations in my house it was our habit to review the merits of neighbors and acquaintances. Ramón Siffoni was one of those who came out of this scrutiny in bad standing. His wife didn't escape condemnation either, because my parents, realists that they were, never made wives out to be victims of their slothful husbands. That she also worked, a very strange thing in our milieu, didn't exempt her, but rather made her all the more suspect. The thin seamstress, so small, so bird-like, neurotic to the highest degree, whose business hours were impossible to determine because she was always gossiping in the doorway—what did she really do? It was a mystery. The mystery was part of the judgment, because my parents, being realists, were aware of the fact that the recompense of work was fickle and too often undeserved. The enigmatic divinity of work was made flesh, in a negative suspension of judgment, in Delia Siffoni. My mother could spot the clothes she made on any woman in town (she certainly knew them all)—they were perfect, insanely neat, above all on Saturday nights when they made their usual rounds and afterward she would mention them to Delia; it seemed a little hypocritical to me, but I didn't really understand her machinations very well. Epiphanies and hypocrisy, after all, are part of the divine plan.

At that precise moment in her professional life, and in her life generally, Delia had fallen into a trap of her own design. Silvia Balero, the drawing teacher, sworn innocent and candidate for spinsterhood, was getting married in a hurry. For appearances' sake she would do it in the church, in white. And the order for the wedding dress was given to Delia. As she was an artist, Balero made the pattern herself—daring, unheard of—and came back from Bahía Blanca, where she often went in her little car, with a ton of tulle and voile, all nylon, which was the latest thing. She even brought the thread to sew it with, also synthetic, with trim in pearl-strewn banlon. Her drawings accounted for the smallest details, and on top of that she made it her business to be present for the cutting and preliminary basting: everybody knew the seamstress had to be watched closely. Now then, Delia was especially prudish, more than most. She was almost malevolent in that sense; for years she had been alert to every moral irregularity in town. And when her acquaintances, the ones she talked to all day, began to ask her questions (because the Balero case was discussed with intense pleasure) she became annoyed and started to make threats—for example, that she would not sew that dress, the gown of white hypocritical infamy ... But of course she would! An order like that came once a year, or less. And with the useless husband that she had—according to the neighborhood consensus, she was not in a position to moralize. The situation was tailored for her, because one velocity was superimposed on another. I already said that when she put her hands to a job the fittings overlapped with the final stitch ... A pregnancy had a fixed term and speed, which is to say, a certain slowness; but this was not a matter of a baby's layette; in Silvia Balero's case it was an anachronism of timing, which attracted a lot of attention in town. The ceremony, the white dress, the husband ... It all had to be carried out quickly, in an instant, in the blink of an eye, that was the only way it would work. And it didn't really work, because anyone who might claim an opinion that would matter to Silvia was already on notice. It's something to think about, why she went to so much trouble. Probably because she was obligated to do it.

She was a girl whose twentieth year had passed without a fiancé, without marriage. She was a professional, in her way. She had studied drawing, or something like that, in an academy in Bahía Blanca; she taught classes at the nun's school (her job was in jeopardy), at the National College, and to private students; she organized exhibitions, and that kind of thing. She was not only a licensed drawing teacher but a friend of the arts, she was almost avant-garde. It was true she'd gotten only as far as the Impressionists, but there's no need to be too harsh on that point. For Pringlenses at that time you had to explain Impressionism, and start history all over again, with courage. She did not lack courage, even if perhaps it was only her foolish thoughtlessness. And she was pretty, very pretty even, a tall blonde with marvelous green eyes, but that is what always happens to spinsters: being pretty to no effect. To have been pretty in vain.

The real problem was not her, but the husband. Who could it be? It was a mystery. It takes two to get married. She was getting married, for love, as they said (or they made her say in the stories: everything was very indirect), and not out of necessity ... very well, it was a lie but very well. Except, to whom? Because the subject, the responsible party, was married, and had three daughters. Hysterics of the type who took their nuptial fantasies for reality were abundant among the spinsters of Pringles. They represented an almost magical power. And from Balero one might well expect something like that, even if no one had expected it of her before. This was all supposition, commentary, gossip, but it was advisable to pay attention to it because as a general rule that was as right as the truth.

7

DELIA SIFFONI WAS already crazy, and the disappearance of her only son drove her crazy again. She went into a frenzy. Prodigious spectacle, perennial postcard, transcendental cinema, scene of scenes: to see a madwoman go mad. It's like seeing God. The history of the last decades has made this occasion stranger and stranger. Although I was a witness, I would not dare attempt a description. I defer to the judgment of the neighborhood, where the members of the same sex as the defendant always got the last word. The men were in charge of the men, the women of the women. My mother was an enthusiastic supporter of desperation when it came to children. According to her, there was nothing to do but howl, lose your head, make scenes. Luckily she never had to: she had German blood, she was discreet and reserved in the extreme, and I don't know how she would have managed it. Anything less was equivalent to being "calm," which in her allusive but very precise language meant not loving your offspring. Beyond desperation she saw nothing. Later she did see, she saw too much, when our happiness fell apart, but at that time she was very strict: the scene, the curtain of screaming—and beyond it nothing. The fact was, neither she nor any woman she knew had ever had to go mad with anguish; life was not very novelistic then... The madness of a mother could only be unleashed, hypothetically, by some horrendous accident to her children. And everything happened to us—we were free, savage children—but not the definitively horrendous. We didn't get lost, we didn't disappear... How could we get lost in a town where everyone knew each other, and almost everyone was more or less related? A child could only be lost in labyrinths and they didn't exist among us. Even so, it did exist if only as a fear, the accident existed: an invisible force dragged the accident toward reality, and kept dragging at it even there, giving it the most capricious forms, reordering over and over its details and circumstances, creating it, annihilating it, with all the unmatched power of fiction. There lay the happiness of Pringles, and there it must still lie.

It can't seem strange, then, that in the midst of that ordeal Delia saw herself before the abyss, before the magnetic field of the abyss, and she rushed forward. What else could she do?

8

THE ABYSS THAT opened before Delia Siffoni had (and still has) a name: Patagonia. When I tell the French I come from there (barely lying) they open their mouths with admiration, almost with incredulity. There are a lot of people all over the world who dream of traveling some day to Patagonia, that extreme end of the planet, a beautiful and inexpressible desert, where any adventure might happen. They're all more or less resigned to never getting that far, and I have to admit they're right. What would they go there to do? And how would they get there, anyway? All the seas and cities are in the way, all the time, all the adventures. It's true that tour companies simplify trips quite a bit these days, but for some reason I keep thinking that going to Patagonia is not so easy. I see it as something quite different from any other trip. My life was carried to Patagonia on a gust of wind, in a moment, that day in my childhood, and it stayed there. I don't think traveling is worth the trouble if you don't bring your life along with you.

It's something I'm confirming at my own expense during these melancholy days in Paris. It's paradoxical, but a journey is bearable only if it's insignificant, if it doesn't count, if it doesn't leave a mark. A person travels, goes to the other side of the world, but leaves his life packed away at home, ready to be recovered on his return. But when he's far away he wonders if perhaps he might have brought his life with him by accident, and left nothing at home. The doubt is enough to create an atrocious fear, unbearable above all because it is a baseless fear, a melancholy.

There's always a reason given for rushing into things. That's what reasons are for. The one Delia used was not only correct in itself but also appropriate for what had happened, along general lines, leaving some details aside. That day at noon, just when we were playing in the street, Chiquito had set out in his truck for Comodoro Rivadavia, carrying I don't know what, probably wool. My Aunt Alicia, who rented him a room in her house, had seen him leave, after an early lunch she'd prepared for him. He'd filled the tank in the morning to prepare for the crossing and then climbed into the truck after lunch, started the engine and left in a hurry. What could be more natural than that a boy playing in the empty box might be imprisoned by the movement, fail to make himself heard, and be carried by accident to who-knew-where—a perfectly involuntary kidnapping? It was unlikely the truck driver would stop before nightfall, and by then he would already be past the Río Negro, well into Patagonia. Chiquito's endurance was formidable, he was a bull, and in this case he'd even made some comment (and if he hadn't made it, Alicia could well have invented it) about how urgently they were waiting for that shipment and how convenient it was to leave after a good lunch and make a long haul all at once, etc.

Several hours had already passed, and the whole neighborhood was on tenterhooks over the case of the lost boy. Mr. Siffoni had taken the matter in hand, although it might have been only to diminish his wife's hysteria. As soon as the boy went missing a crisis was set off by the supposition of a forced departure in the truck's cab or trailer, which was not entirely unreasonable. It was almost too obvious. The neighbor women were a little guilty of presenting it that way to Delia. Next they did something absolutely unheard-of: they called a taxi, so as not to lose another minute going after the truck. In Pringles there were two taxis, and they were only used for going to the Roca train station. One of them, Zaralegui's, had to be called by phone. He must not really have understood the matter at hand, or he wouldn't have undertaken the trip. It was absurd, since his 1930s Chrysler could never reach the cruising speed of a truck a quarter of a century more modern. But they didn't think it was strange for the pursuer to be slower than the pursued. On the contrary, it seemed that by the logic of the long term it would have to catch up—what else could happen?

In the rush of departure, Delia, who was acting like a lunatic, snatched up her sewing kit and the wedding dress she was working on, thinking she could keep working during the journey, because the job was so urgent. Now, if that was the case, if the work was urgent, the neighbors might wonder, why didn't she work, instead of spending the day keeping up with everything in the street? She was out of her mind at that critical moment: an enormous wedding dress with a vaporous white train and a volume exceeding her own (which was pretty meager) was the most awkward thing she could have chosen to bring. (I want to make a note here of an idea that may be useful later on: the only appropriate mannequin I can think of for a wedding dress is a snowman.) Besides, sewing a wedding dress in the back of a taxi, bouncing along those dirt roads that go south ... Where would her famous meticulousness end?

And she left, like a crazy woman ... The neighbors saw her go and stayed where they were, commenting and awaiting her return: The situation was so irrational they really thought she would be back at any minute. She hadn't even locked up the house, she hadn't even let her husband know ... That was enough to justify the neighbor women staying there on the sidewalk in a circle, gossiping and waiting for Ramon Siffoni so they could tell him his wife had left, desperate, crazy (like a good mother), and still wasn't back ...

All this may seem very surreal, but that's not my fault. I realize it seems like an accumulation of absurd elements, in keeping with the surrealist method, a way of attaining a scene of pure invention without the work of inventing it. Breton and his friends brought elements together from anywhere, from the most distant places; in fact they preferred them as far flung as possible, so that the surprise would be greater, the effect more effective. It's interesting to observe that in their search for the distant they went—for example, in the "exquisite corpses"—only to what was closest at hand: the colleague, the friend, the wife. For my part, I don't go near or far, because I'm not looking for anything. It's as if everything had already happened. And, in fact, it did all happen; but at the same time it's as if it hadn't happened, as if it were happening now. Which is to say, as if nothing had happened.

9

DURING THE TAXI ride Delia didn't sew a stitch or open her mouth. She rode along stiffly in the back seat with her gaze fixed on the road, hoping against hope that she would see the truck. Zaralegui didn't say anything either, but his silence had a different density, because it was the last afternoon of his life. He could have said his last words, but he kept them to himself. He concentrated on driving; though the traffic on the road didn't demand much attention (there was none), the potholes did. He was a good professional. He must have been intrigued, or at least confused, by what was happening. No one had ever taken him on such an inexplicable trajectory before, and he must have been wondering how far, how long.... He wouldn't wonder much longer, poor man, because very soon he was going to die.

What happened was that, many hours down the road, an enormous truck suddenly hurled itself into them, into Zaralegui at the wheel, in front. Except that the truck was smashed not in front, but behind. Or rather they were the ones who hurled themselves into the truck, and at full speed, at the multiplied speed that only occurs when two vehicles collide head-on. Who knows how it could have happened, since they were both going in the same direction. Maybe the truck had reduced its speed a little, a very little, and this was equivalent to a fantastic acceleration on the part of the car coming up from behind. (To explain this episode to myself, as with so many others, I am assuming, not very realistically, enormous speeds.) What's certain is that the Chrysler was smashed against the back of the tractor trailer in the most savage manner—was destroyed, reduced to a shell of crushed tin. And not only that: it stuck there, like a meteorite that had collided with a planet, and it continued its travels, suspended. The truck driver, ninety feet ahead, didn't even notice. Those trucks really were like planets. Anyone driving one would never know what was happening at its unreachable extremities—especially pulling a trailer, like another planet rolling along behind.

Zaralegui died instantly; he had no time to think anything. Delia, who was riding in the back, busy attaching a bodice with her miniscule stitches, was unscathed. But the crash, the jolt, the adhesion to the planet, and Zaralegui's backwards leap, which brought him to rest in her arms like a baby, already dead, in a rosebud of tulle, produced a considerable shock. She lost consciousness and continued the journey asleep, without seeing the landscape. It was more of an hysterical coma than sleep, and she emerged from it a different woman, gone crazy for the third time. She never knew it, but the truck driver had parked on the side of the road and slept all night in his bunk bed, the little compartment those trucks have behind the cab, and then resumed the trip at dawn and didn't stop the whole next day.

When Delia awoke, the sun was setting over the province of Santa Cruz.

10

PATAGONIA . . . the end of the world . . . yes, agreed; but the end of the world is still the world. The whole pink sky, like the petal of a colossal flower, the blue earth, an immobile disk with no other end but the horizon . . . That was the world, then. That was the whole world, that place where Delia had been taken by accident, by the mad force of events, and from which it seemed entirely unthinkable that she would ever escape. At first she felt like a child on a carousel, riding on the back of a beetle made of black glass. She even thought she heard music; and she did, actually, but it was the whistling of the wind.

Then, all at once, the horrible circumstances of which she was victim and protagonist became clear to her. She let out a scream and waved her arms in terror, at which Zaralegui's corpse abandoned her lap and flew out of the car. A pothole must have helped: she wasn't that strong.

And in addition to the potholes, in all certainty, the maelstrom of wind—at full speed the truck displaced a mass of air the volume and weight of a mountain. The mountains missing from that infinite plateau were created by the air. But there was also wind, and more than a little: Patagonia is the land of wind. In fact there were various winds, which competed for the dust raised by the truck and fought fiercely with the vehicle's own wind, packed and wrapped by speed. They unwrapped this package a thousand times a second with a sound like paper in the air, they untied the ribbons of gravity, they tore up in their hurry, like children driven by the sight of toys, both its rigid and fluid folds.

Zaralegui gave two half-somersaults twelve feet in the air; no acrobat in the world could have imitated his pirouettes with the broken spine that he had. Then he went flying off to one side. Since his arms were moving, agitated by the same force that carried him, he seemed alive. What a spectacle! But the conjunction of the pothole and the whirlwind must have made a catapult, because Zaralegui wasn't the only one who flew: he was followed by the dress, Delia, and the car, in that order. When the dress opened the enormous white wings of its train and rose, at a supersonic velocity, up and away, Delia felt dispossessed. It was her work that was going, and she was left out, useless. She thought she'd never get it back. And then when Delia herself took flight, all her feelings contracted into terror. It was the first time she flew.

The earth dropped away, the truck too—(the last she saw of it was the back wall of the trailer, from which the black cocoon that had been the Chrysler was coming loose, to take its turn at flying)—the sky approached vertiginously. She closed her eyes and after an instant opened them again.

The sun, which had already set on the surface, appeared again at the end of the world; it was the first time she'd seen the sun after it had set. It was as red as a red rubber ball slick with luminous oil. And it was in a strange place: although visible, it stayed below the line of the horizon, in a niche. It was the nighttime sun, which no one had ever seen.

And it's not as if Delia lingered in contemplation of the sun. It couldn't even be said that she looked at it. She wasn't even thinking, and thinking always comes before looking. Flying was an absorbing activity for her—so much so, and so absorbing of life, that she was absolutely convinced she would not survive. And how could she? The contradictory currents of the wind had carried her, in two or three somersaults, to a height of more than a hundred yards. The circle of the horizon changed position as if the compass had fallen into the hands of a lunatic. The winds seemed to be shouting berserkly: "You take her! ... Give her here!"—amid uncanny bursts of laughter. Delia was thrown back and forth, vibrating, vibrating, like a heart in the heights and depths of love, or in space.

"These are my last moments," she screamed to herself without moving her lips. The last seconds of her life, and afterward there would be only the black night of death ... Her anguish was unspeakable. Talking in terms of seconds was rhetoric, but it was also a great truth. The mad winds seemed bold enough to turn the seconds into minutes, and even hours, and if they felt like it, it would not be out of place to say days. But even so they would be seconds, because anguish compresses time, whatever interval of time, to the painful dimensions of seconds.

I should at least take advantage of this experience, she managed to say to herself, since there won't be another one to follow it.

But that was, from any point of view, impossible. Enjoyment is impossible when everything is impossible; what's more, there was no point of view; the show she was putting on didn't have a point of view, since there was no one to see it. There in the limpid heights of twilight, she spun around so many times at a speed greater than sound, that she no longer had relative positions. She was a collage, a figure cut out and moved by a capricious artist, filmed in fast-forward against the pinkest and smoothest backdrop in the world (or in the sky) and illuminated by a red spotlight. No one enjoys the experience immediately before death, ever. Although, of course, with death, the quintessentially unexpected, no experience can be called the last. There's always the possibility that it's the next-to-last. This was an error on Delia's part (her last moments!), the first of a strange series that would carry her very far.

Some things seem eternal, and still they pass anyway. Death itself does that. Delia had lost sight of the earth a little while before, and she no longer knew if she was moving forward or backward, falling or rising, following the vertical or the horizontal... What did it matter, at that point? There was always a new wind to take hold of her and play yo-yo with her. Where did they come from, those winds? The torrent seemed to come from a hole in the sky—the hole was invisible.

But, as I say, suddenly it was over. Delia found herself on the earth again, and walking. She really didn't know how it happened. But, there she was walking on her two legs, on the flat, clean-swept earth. She didn't see a tree, a hill, anything. She forgot immediately the danger of death she had just faced.

Delia loved to play the committed fatalist, the lady of death—every afternoon she felt prepared to spend the night at a wake; her conversations were full of cancer, blindness, paralysis, comas, heart attacks, widows, orphans. She had embodied this character with so much enthusiasm that it was now her theme, her position. It was an inclination she had chosen, because the safe and protected life she'd led, the cocoon of the small town middle class, placed her on the margin of any serious test in which her survival could be at stake. Her desire to live was exempt from any corroboration. And this also formed a part of her definitive being. While she flew, with no time to think or react (which are the same thing), she had clung to her old philosophy. Yet now that she was walking, safe and sound, time was opening up beneath her feet; her legs were the scissors that cut the translucent stalk of time and continuously opened and unfolded it. And because of this she saw before her the urgent necessity to give way to certain ideas about reality and to renounce momentarily that "what does it matter, I'm dead already anyway" that constituted her elegance.

She didn't know where she was or where she was headed—or even what time it was. To start with, how was it possible that it was daytime? It was night, she felt that in her body and her mind. And yet, it was day. What insane zone had she fallen into?

Then this is Patagonia? she said to herself, perplexed. And if this is Patagonia, then what am I?

11

MEANWHILE, WHEN NIGHT had almost fallen, Ramón Siffoni returned to the neighborhood in his little red truck and found a committee of anguish waiting for him.

"Omar wasn't lost!" he began, but he stopped there, because he sensed that no one was listening. He was a nervous and bad-tempered man, impatient, demanding and dissatisfied. "Where's my wife?" he asked.

This was what the neighbors were waiting for.

"She took a taxi to Patagonia."

If they'd bored a hole in the back of his neck with a drill they couldn't have shaken him more badly.

They explained it to him, but who knows if anything got through his crust of rage. But something must have gotten through, because he got back into his red wreck of a truck and took off with a noise like rattling tin cans—also headed south, where everyone seemed to be going that day.

What he didn't see was parked on the corner—a little sky-blue one-seater car, the kind that had to be dismantled from the top for the driver to get in: it began to follow him. Such a maneuver was highly unusual, perhaps the first, and the last time, such a thing happened in Pringles.

And even so, it went unnoticed. The neighbor women were dazzled by the abrupt gesture, romantic in its way, of the angry husband. And Ramón Siffoni . . . what could he notice, in his state? He ran, he launched himself off, to keep his wife from committing the greatest mistake of her life. And if his old red truck was not as fast as it needed to be, it didn't matter, because what he wanted at that moment was an interplanetary rocket ship.

He was going, as anyone with a map can verify, southeast. Which is to say, in the two directions that lengthen the day in the Argentine summer. And as he was beside himself, he was the southeast. That worked. The day began to lengthen like a snake, and the red truck, which in the immensities it now slid across was becoming truly small, was the blazing hungry head of the snake, with its tongue sticking out: the tongue was the crank with its two right angles which in his haste Ramón had forgotten to take off.

12

BUT HE WAS not alone. A half mile or so behind, the gaze of a lady at the wheel was fixed on his trail of dust, driving a little sky-blue car, one of the smallest and lightest ever constructed. The fact that it was as light as a yawn mattered less (or didn't matter at all) in view of the important mystery the little car held. That was everything. That little car was the mystery, and it was more than that: it was mystery in motion. Those vehicles, made for mobility in cities, for short distances, were an eccentricity of the fifties and sixties, and forgotten afterwards. We called them "mice." Only one not very fat person fit, and only if they were tightly folded-up. No one ever thought of traveling in one of those cars. And yet this one, a pale blue example of the tiniest model, threw itself into the longest and most dangerous chase, almost like a miniature replica of something else—a toy intruding into the adult world. Surrounding it, Patagonia, gigantic and deserted, was beginning to open its vast mouth. But the car was not afraid. It pressed on, at full speed, almost as if it knew where it was going, or as if it were going somewhere. Or as if it were not going anywhere. It was the magnet-car, the soda bubble in the wind, the blue point of the sky, mystery in all its dimensions. The proverb says mystery does not occupy space. All right, fine; but it crosses it.

13

VERY WELL. NOW all the protagonists in the adventure are on stage. Let me see if I can make an orderly list:

1) The huge tractor trailer, Chiquito's double planet, leading the way.

2) The shell of Zaralegui's Chrysler, at this point looking more than anything like a black lacquered Chinese bathtub.

3) Zaralegui's corpse.

4) Delia Siffoni, lost and wandering around.

5) Silvia Balero's wedding dress, carried by the wind.

6) Ramón Siffoni in his red truck (a day behind).

7) And closing the retinue, the mysterious little blue car.

Of course, it's not that simple. There are other characters, who are now going to appear . . . Or better yet, no. It's not that there are other characters (these are all of them) but revelations will transform these characters into others, making room for encounters that Delia Siffoni never would have expected, neither she nor any of the other Delia Siffonis in the world, with all of them beginning, there in Patagonia, a dance of transformations.

There are drunks who, starting at a certain point in the evening, sample all kinds of mixes: they drink anything, a glass of any alcohol at hand, at random. We know how imprudent this policy is, but they laugh and keep going; you have to recognize their astonishing physical vigor, their superhuman stamina, which they might have been born with but which they've certainly developed further with this habit—the paradox of self-destruction, which conversely never quite arrives. They mix everything, and they don't worry ... it all contributes to the same effect, which is inebriation, their personal inebriation, which is singular, unique. And if he also is singular, the drinker says to himself, what does it matter how many elements there are to take him to that sublime level of unity ...

Happy drunk! If he's gotten that far, he's gotten to everything, he has no reason to worry anymore, because the idea on which he bases all his reasoning is correct, and there's nothing else to say (even though it's bad for your health). It's true that he is singular, and it's true that this is a process of simplification: everything goes toward a kind of happy nothing, and nothing is lost on the way.

"Simplify, child, simplify." For some reason, I can't do it. I want to, but I can't. It's stronger than I am. It's as if I were abstemious. Here in Paris I drink more than I should.

As I am not much of a drinker, the effect is immediate, and exaggerated. It's the effect and nothing but. The effect is to walk drunkenly, smiling stupidly past all those prestigious places, accumulating experiences, memories, for a time when I have nothing else to lean on. It's a commonplace to say that a great city offers a continuous succession of different impressions, all in a magma of variable intensity. But shouldn't it also be true for other people, not just for oneself? I see people pass, from café terraces where I write, and all without exception look compact, closed in on themselves, making it very clear that the city has had no effect on them.

But what am I after? I don't know. People disarmed by their own visions, like Picasso's women, medusa-like and limping, thousand-armed goddesses, hollow people, fluid people?

Maybe what I hope to see, at the end of a line of self-sustaining reasoning, is people who, like myself, have no life. In that, I am condemned to failure. It's curious, but everyone has life, even the tourists, who by my reasoning shouldn't. No one leaves life anywhere, all lives seem to be portable. They are naturally so. To be practical about it and drop the metaphysics, having a life is equivalent to having business, affairs, interests. And how can anyone strip himself of all that? Very well. But then how did I do it?

I don't know.

I've stood on the threshold of all the beauties, all the dangers. And the sums did not add up. The remainders did not remain, the multiplications were not multiplied, the divisions were not divided.

14

LET'S SUPPOSE A man who, as a result of a mental disturbance (I can imagine this because yesterday I saw it), cannot walk, advance, or move at all, without the accompaniment or propulsion of very sonorous music, which he is obliged to provide for himself at the top of his lungs. Uncomfortable for other people, evidently; but maybe not as much as you'd think, at least for those who see him only briefly and think, quite reasonably, that the poor unhappy man isn't doing it because he likes to. It's curious, because I'd bet that anyone who has to put up with him every day would certainly have the right to think he does do it because he likes it, and surely they do think that. Because he could always choose immobility and keep quiet.

He moves not in silence, but in song. It's almost like opera: the song becomes gesture, and fate, and plot (incoherent, insane), and the people who surround him also become destiny and fate.

He advances loaded down with signifiers, dragging the cart of his rhythm, which only he perceives. He opens a pathway by opening his life with the demented clumsiness of an angry man tearing the gift wrap off a present. But he doesn't find a gift, and keeps on opening forever, singing forever. The perpetual melodrama. There it is, what his accusers may wonder: Why does he insist? Actually, they wonder what comes first: movement or song? Does he sing to walk, or walk to sing? All right, there is no answer, as there is none for the puzzle of the opera. Because there is no anterior or posterior, there is no succession, only a kind of successive simultaneity.

It was within this strange logic that Delia Siffoni walked through Patagonia that calamitous afternoon. But she didn't walk with the obliviousness of the madman. The poor woman had fallen into the trap of a melodrama where she was just another character, and barely that—Delia Siffoni, the woman who was always talking about disasters. Her fatalist palinodes wouldn't have helped her now, because fate did not depend on her. She was in an ensemble, but she was all alone. There was no third person. There was no story.

How could this happen to me? she said to herself. How could I have come to land, without realizing it, in this stony, godforsaken desert? She meant: to me, why did it have to happen to me and not to someone else? She belonged to a common type: without ever really thinking it over in detail, she had considered herself a woman like the rest, with no reason for anything to happen to her that didn't also happen to all other women. It was as if this sort of thing happened to someone else, to an absolute someone else, which is to say, as if it didn't happen to anyone. And yet . . .

Her brain, somewhat feverish at that moment, was unexpectedly reviewing all kinds of exceptions. She knew so many women who were victims of lamentable fates, some of them almost unbelievable in their bitterness. So many women who could have asked themselves "Why me?" ... and the question was left unanswered ... So many, that suddenly it seemed as if it were all of them. In that sense then, she, to whom nothing ever happened, was part of a small minority of typical women, so small she was almost alone in it. Inconceivable women who were free to narrate it all, to fill themselves with all destinies. And if she was the exception, the only one, if the world was turned around in that sense, then it was logical that the exceptional and unique would happen to her. Just to her. Maybe it seemed like there were so many victims because she had always devoted herself to their disasters, to juicy remarks, one after another, squeezing the last drops out of them. She was grandly unoccupied, she was the gossip woman. For example, something was coming back to her, who knows why, with almost excessive microscopic clarity—the case of a young woman who in the recent past had been one of her favorite topics until it was displaced by the electrifying Balero affair: the girl was named Cati Prieto, she had been married for a couple of years and was the mother of a baby; the husband, with the excuse (justified or not, that was unknown) of a job in Suárez, had literally abandoned her; he came Sunday mornings, he left at night, he didn't even stay to sleep. He had another woman in Suárez, that was obvious. And when he presented himself, the bastard, hardly noticing the presence of his son, she spent the hours pointing out the child's progress to him, the smile, the little hand, the gurgling; look, did you see, did you hear ... and him smoking through it all, behind his mask of ice, his indifference. And she would insist, the poor unhappy girl . . . papá, pa . . . pá . . . For the commentators on the case, like Delia, it was relatively simple, because in the end it all came down to an unknown quantity, like when people say, "Every family is a world," and no one can pretend to know an entire world. But maybe . . . this occurred to Delia now, with the crystalline clarity of her vision . . . maybe the pathetic young girl didn't know either. She didn't know either, to start with, if her husband had abandoned her or not, if she was stupid, if she was hanging on to her hopes, if he did or did not have another woman in Suárez, et cetera. Maybe she didn't know anything, and maybe she had no way of knowing it; she was the one who knew the least, like when they say, "She's always the last to know," and that's where the gossips made their mistake: believing that the sea of ignorance they operated over was a mirage, until their wings were broken and they found themselves thrashing in waters that were real and turbulent and salty. Cursed water, that does not satisfy thirst.

Cursed Patagonia, beautiful and diabolical. Her anguish and perplexity grew with every passing minute. Like all housewives, of each and every epoch, Delia was very stuck on schedules, a slave to them even when she thought she was their master. And here it seemed as if schedules did not exist, directly. The day went on. It actually scared her a little. Strange atmospheric phenomena seemed to be occurring: a curtain of clouds had risen from the horizon, and in the heights of the sky there were disordered movements . . . While on the surface reigned an astonishing calm. That by itself was strange, threatening, and together with the persistence of the light, the calm was beginning to give the castaway chills. She couldn't believe this was happening to her. She couldn't, and now she hardly tried; but still she felt that it had happened, or was happening, enough to make her believe it, and leave behind her smooth and flat reality, her life of schedules.

Where could I be? she wondered.

The belief had a name: Patagonia.

The circumstances made Delia practical. Goodbye to her funereal philosophies, her fantasies of a housewife in black! Suddenly there were more urgent matters to resolve. The simple fact of being alive and not dead had unexpected consequences. How simple the causes are, how complicated the effects!

She had to find shelter. A place to spend the night. Because the night, which had not yet come, would waste no time arriving, and then she would really be in trouble. Much more than she imagined, even though it would be precisely what she was imagining: a night without a moon, without light, everything transformed into horrors ... That was what was beyond her imagination: the nature of the transformations. Because she saw nothing around her that could be susceptible to turning into something else, not a tree, not a rock ... The clouds? She couldn't conceive of being afraid of a cloud. And as for the air, it wasn't susceptible to taking shapes.

But still, there were things there. She wasn't in the ether. The faltering afterglow at the end of the long twilight was there, showing her millions of objects: grasses, thistles, pebbles, clods of earth, anthills, bones, shells of armadillos, dead birds, stray feathers, ants, beetles ...

And the great gray plateau.

15

WHAT DELIA DIDN'T know, in that endless twilight, was that there was a night in this story of hers. She was unaware of it because she'd spent it in a coma inside the remains of the Chrysler smashed against the truck-planet.

Ramón Siffoni, her husband, had driven all night in his little red truck without giving himself a minute's rest. He didn't even think of stopping to sleep for a while, not at all. He saw the moon rise before him, an orange disk gushing light, and he felt like the master of the hours and the nights, of all of them without exceptions or interruptions, in a perfect continuum. His concentration at the wheel was perfect too. The night had arrived in the midst of this concentration, while the truck passed like a toy through the sleeping towns. Suddenly it was the desert, and suddenly it was night. The towns became jumbled arrangements of stones, the kind that radiated darkness. The cities rose out of the earth.

They were not cities: no one lived in them. But they resembled cities as one drop of water resembles another. The fact that there was no one in them only meant that no one had to orient themselves on their rough escarpments. Their streets ran according to a general abstract orientation, like the map of the moon. It was when he was crossing the Río Colorado that the moon came out, over the bridge, and Ramón was mesmerized, his eyes like two stars. A great unknown plateau had placed itself between him and the horizon, taking the place of his concentration. There was nothing there.

A phenomenon had taken place without him knowing it, a phenomenon that was unrecorded but very common in Patagonia: the atmospheric tides. The full moon, exercising the entire attractive force of its mass over the landscape, draws the sleeping atoms out of the earth and makes them undulate in the air. Not just atoms, which wouldn't count for much, but their particles too, among them those of light and the extremely intricate ones of order.

Maybe the tide that night had some effect on Siffoni's brain, maybe not, we'll never know. For the truck, it had the curious consequence of depriving it of its color, the red it had had when it left the factory forty years ago and which was now half-faded, though it still shone so brightly at daybreak in the summer, when the birds were singing. And also the color under the paint. It turned transparent, although there was nobody to see it.

When, hours later, Ramón looked in the rearview mirror, he saw a little blue car following along a half-mile behind him. The dust had turned transparent too. The presence there of the tiny vehicle filled him with uneasiness. The uneasiness made him feel pursued. A short while later, they were still separated by the same distance. It didn't seem difficult to lose the car; he had never seen a car as tiny as that one before, and he doubted it had much of an engine. He accelerated. He would have thought it impossible, because he had the accelerator pressed to the floor already, but nonetheless the truck sped up, by a lot. It shot forward, the little glass truck, like an arrow shot from a bow.

Here I digress. Because, thinking it over, the moon did have an effect on Ramón. It was that he saw himself as a husband. He was a husband like so many, regularly good, and normal, more or less. But what he now saw was that this comfortable role in which he found himself rested entirely on one supposition, which was "I could be worse." Indeed, there are husbands who beat their wives, or debase them in this or that way and humiliate them, or play all kinds of dirty tricks on them, in general very visibly (nothing is more visible for those contemplating a marriage), all of which culminates in abandonment: there are husbands who leave, who vanish like smoke, lots of them. So even if the husband stays, and persists in his infamies, even so, he "could be worse." He could leave. But women are not so foolish as to go along with this scenario; it's evidently "better to be alone than in bad company," since there are life-threatening situations in which getting rid of a monstrous husband is better than keeping him. Actually the "could be worse" premise is very flexible, and even very demanding; the least flaw could discredit a husband in the eyes of his wife. "He could be worse ..." only if he is already almost perfect, if his faults are venial, of the humorous type (for example if he doesn't pull his pants up a half an inch every time he sits down, so that after a while the fabric stretches at the knees). Very well, in this way a hierarchy is established: there are men who are monsters and make life hell for their wives, like drunks, for example; and there are others who don't, and if a husband is in the latter category he can allow himself the luxury of looking back over his small (and large) defects, sitting in his easy chair in the living room and reading the paper while his wife makes dinner, and feel very sure of himself. So sure of himself that pretty soon he sees opening in front of him, like a marvelous flower, the world of vices that he could, that he can, practice with impunity thanks to his position as a good husband, a good family man. Life allows him this, it's for him and only him. Wouldn't it be a shame, a crime, to waste an opportunity like that? The specter of dirty tricks is his Jacob's ladder: each step will have its subtle dialectic of "I could be worse," and a lifetime won't be long enough for him to reach the top, the monster.

Well then, Ramón Siffoni had a vice. He was a gambler. Marriage had made him a gambler, but the game had made him a married man as well. He'd gambled long before he got married, since his early youth, but in the case of gambling, like all vices, it wasn't so much a matter of starting as of continuing. He was incorrigible. With him it was definitive. It was the mark of his life, the stigma. He gambled everything, the money he earned and what his wife earned too, in the form of undeferrable debts: the furniture, the house (luckily they rented), and the truck. He was always broke, strapped, and he sank from there to vertiginous depths. He always lost, like all true gamblers. It was a miracle that they survived, that they fed and dressed themselves and paid their bills and raised their son. The secret must have been that at times, by chance, he won, and with the marvelous imprudence of gamblers, who never think about tomorrow, he would spend all the winnings, down to the last cent, on catching up and getting on with things: so that the same gesture of short-sightedness that at night acted against the family, acted in its favor in the daytime. More miraculous, much more, was that it wasn't known in the neighborhood, in the town (all of Pringles was one neighborhood, and information circulated as fast as a body in free fall). Of course activities of that kind are carried on with a certain discretion; but even so, it's inconceivable that it wasn't found out, that my mother, an intimate of Delia's, didn't know. Because, although discreet and nocturnal, it was a pastime obviously subject to indiscretions. And it had been going on for years, and it would continue for decades, before and after (before and after what?). And above all, it would have taken very little, any fact, the tiniest filament of information, to draw conclusions, for the whole thing to be explained ... And even so, it was only found out many years later (clearly it was found out, otherwise I wouldn't be writing this), I was no longer living in Pringles, one day, I'm not sure when, on one of my visits, Mamá knew it, she knew it very well, she was tired of knowing it, how else would the vicissitudes, the status quo of the Siffoni family be explained, without that piece of information? How would it have been explained from the beginning, from our prehistory in the neighborhood? That's what I wonder: How? If no one knew!

The stakes are always raised. The moon was rising ... But it was not rising, just as the sun does not rise; the ascent is an illusion created by the turning of the earth... At the zenith of the betting, Ramón Siffoni, the moon-man, who by the mere gravitation of his mass made the tides of money rise, would lay on the table, or had already laid on the table, the supreme bet: his marriage.

When he looked in the mirror again, the little blue car was still following him, pegged at a distance of one half mile. Ramón gave more credence now to his suspicion that they were following him. What to do? Accelerating more was useless, and could be counterproductive. He took his foot off the gas pedal and let his speed fall by itself; he always did that, it was an automatic thing. From a hundred it dropped to ninety, eighty, seventy... sixty... fifty, forty, thirty... My God! It was worse than just slamming on the brakes. The lunar landscape of the plateau had been fleeing past him, and now it fled forward, the transparent dust he was raising over the dirt road surrounded him like quicksilver... It was almost like advancing and retreating in the dimensions, not on the plateau. But when he glanced in the mirror again, there was the half mile, the sky-blue mouse...

He accelerated again, like a lunatic: thirty, forty, fifty, sixty, seventy ... eighty ... ninety, a hundred, a hundred and ten, a hundred and twenty ... the transparency had trouble keeping up with him, the moon leapt ... The truck was crossing its own wake of dust, its own trajectory...

When he looked in the mirror again ... he couldn't believe it. But he had to surrender to the evidence. The little car was there, always at the same distance, the same half mile, which was, what's more, the exact same half mile, not another, equivalent one. He resolved to slow down again, but this time so abruptly that his pursuer would have no choice but to overtake him. That's what he did: a hundred, ninety, eighty, seventy, sixty, fifty, forty... thirty... twenty, ten, zero, minus ten, minus twenty, minus thirty ... —he had never done that before. The whirlwinds of the moon enveloped him.

And still, when he looked in the rearview mirror, to his immense surprise, there was the blue car, and the half mile that separated them. He accelerated. He decelerated. Etc. If he hadn't believed it at first, now at the end of a couple of hours of racing, he was even less able to believe it. What most intrigued him, in his periodic inspections of the rearview mirror (which was external, the kind that sticks out on a metal arm from the side of the cab) was that the small blue car shone so brightly, and that it maintained its position as if suspended above the road, as if floating over the potholes while he bounced up and down, and on top of everything that the distance remained identical... too identical ... Without reducing or increasing his speed (by this point having tried so many alternations, he no longer knew which side of excess he was on) he cranked down the window with his left hand. When it was open, with his eyes half-closed against the wind, he put his hand out and brought the tip of his forefinger and thumb, as delicately as the lurching of the truck would allow, to the oval surface of the mirror, and pulled off—pulled off the little sky-blue car! As if it were a little decal stuck there ... He brought it up to his eyes, tilting his head a little to see it by the light of the moon: a butterfly wing, metallic cobalt, the moon brought out that shine that had made it so visible ...

He marveled at having fallen prey to such a baroque illusion, it could only happen to him ... Because what was more, a butterfly wing can get stuck on one part or another of a vehicle in motion, in fact it happens all the time on a road trip, but butterflies smash against the parts of a vehicle that break the air, like the windshield or the radiator! And the mirror faced backward! The only explanation was that in one of the recent decelerations the butterfly had gotten trapped in the change of relative velocities and smashed into it from behind. He opened his fingers, let the wind take the centimeter of sky-blue wing, rolled up the window and did not look in the mirror again.

If he had, he would have been surprised to see that the car was still there, just where its silhouette had been traced by a butterfly wing. Inside the car was Silvia Balero, the drawing teacher, mad with anguish and half asleep. She followed Siffoni's red truck because it was the last thread connecting her to her wedding dress, the seamstress, and she had just seen it disappear before her eyes. The moment when the atmospheric tide made the truck invisible found her in bad shape. Like all candidates for spinsterhood, she was very dependent on her biorhythms, and after midnight she was always, always asleep. Never in her life had she gotten past that hour. Night was an unknown quantity for her; she was a diurnal, impressionistic being. So at midnight, which by a strange coincidence was the moment when the moon acted on the truck, she went on automatic pilot, like a sleepwalker. As if in a nightmare she felt despair as her prey vanished before her eyes. In her state, this disappearing act was the trick that hid all of reality from her.

"I'm hungry," thought Ramón Siffoni, who hadn't had dinner. Up ahead, he saw a kind of little mountain under the moon, and on its peak a hotel. In spite of the hour lights could be seen in the windows on the ground floor, and he thought it was not unlikely that there was a dining room. The supposition became much more plausible when he saw, as he came up to it, several trucks parked in front of the hotel. Any traveler in Argentina knows that where truck drivers stop, one eats well; therefore, one stops.

As soon as he stepped on the ground, a woman came walking toward him, although at the same time she appeared to flee from him. He wasn't sure, because what captured his attention was the little blue car she'd alighted from.

Silvia Balero noticed that he didn't recognize her, even though he opened the door for her on her daily visits to the seamstress. All women must have looked the same to him. He was that kind of man.

"I'm sorry to bother you, heaven knows what you'll think of me, but may I ask you a favor?"

Siffoni looked at her with an expression that seemed impolite but was actually intrigue, because she looked familiar and he didn't know from where.

"Could you walk me in? I mean, as if we were colleagues, traveling salesmen. Since you're going to stay here ... I'm nervous about going in alone."

Finally he reacted and took off toward the door.

"No. I'm just going to have dinner."

"Me too! Then I'm getting back on the road!"

She wondered: Where could he have left the truck? It looked

like he'd climbed out of empty air.

But the door was locked; through the curtains the lobby could be seen, dark and deserted. Ramón took a few steps in front of the building, with the woman following behind. The windows of a room that might have been the dining room also showed a black space on the other side, but from somewhere a few rays of smoky light reached him. Ramón Siffoni retreated a few feet. From the road he'd seen lights on, but now he didn't know from where. He tried to make sense of the structure of the building. He couldn't concentrate because of the perplexity his company was causing him; by the light of the moon, the woman did not look very lucid. Might she be drunk, or crazy? That kind of man is always thinking the worst of women, precisely because they all look the same to him.

The difficulties he encountered were due to the fact that the hotel's floor plan was really unintelligible. It was a hot springs establishment whose ground floor had been adapted to the stone wellsprings in the earth; which, being bedrock, could not be removed.

But finally, coming around a sharp corner, he found himself before a lit window, and could see inside. His surprise was superlative (but his surprise was enormous every time he looked at anything that night). He stood before a scene he knew all too well: the poker table. Now, in a flash, he remembered having heard talk of this hotel, a requisite stop for all gamblers headed south, smugglers, truckers, aviators ... An old hot springs hotel, its clientele extinct, a legendary den. He'd never thought that one day—one night—he'd see it for himself.

Before this spectacle he forgot everything, even the woman who stood on tiptoe behind him to see. The men, the cards, the chips, the glasses of whiskey ... But he didn't forget absolutely everything: there was one thing he noticed. One of the gamblers was from Pringles, and he knew him very well, not only because they were neighbors. He was the one everyone called Chiquito, the truck driver. It meant everything to see him, and understand that the trip had not been in vain, or at least that he hadn't gone the wrong way. If he got what he wanted from him, he wouldn't have to keep going.

He knew perfectly well how to get to a gambling table, even if all the doors were closed. His movements became confident, and Silvia Balero noticed. She followed him. Ramón knocked a few times on the window, and then on the closest door. Before anyone came to open it, he searched in his shirt pocket and pulled out a black mask. He'd had it there for some time, and he hadn't expected to use it so soon. He put it on (it had an elastic band that tightened around the back of the neck). In those days it was common, as it is now, for gamblers in poker dens to hide their identities with masks, so the hotel porter who came to open the door only had to look at him to know what he wanted. They entered. Silvia Balero tugged on his sleeve.

"What do you want?" he snapped. He couldn't believe how inconvenient it was to have a strange woman begging for his attention when he was about to make the bet of his life.

She wanted a place to sleep. She was already half asleep in fact, somnambulant.

Without answering her, Ramón signaled to the porter to guide them, but the man told them they had to speak to the owner of the hotel, who happened to be seated at the card table. So they did. Those present threw an appreciative look at the young teacher, and the porter took her to a room not far from where they were and came back. The new arrival was already in place, they had recited the rules for him, and he was requesting chips on credit. Counting the owner, there were five of them. The porter watched. Two were truck drivers, Chiquito and another suspicious-looking man; the remaining two were local ranchers, cattle men, very solvent. Chiquito had won a lot. At that hour they were already playing for thousands of sheep, and entire mountains.

Why linger over a description of a game, the same as any other? Queen, king, two, etc. Ramón lost, successively, his truck, the little blue car, and Silvia Balero. The only thing left was to pay for the two whiskeys he'd drunk. He dropped the cards on the table with his eyes half-closed behind his mask and said:

"Where's the bathroom?"

They pointed it out. He went, and escaped through the window. He ran toward the place where he'd left the truck, pulling the keys out of his pocket ... But when he came to his spot among the other trucks in the lot, all of them big and modern (and Chiquito's, which he knew well, with a strange black machine stuck to the back wall of the trailer; he didn't stop to see what it was) there, on the flat ground, he didn't find his truck. He thought he was dreaming. The moon had disappeared as well, and all that was left was an uncertain brilliance between the earth and the sky. His truck was not there. When he'd bet it, the second trucker, who was the one who'd won, went out to see it, and on returning had accepted the bet against ten thousand sheep, which had surprised Siffoni a little. Could he have moved it then? Impossible without the keys, which had never left his pocket. At any rate he couldn't look for it for very long, because discovery of his escape was imminent... He tried to get into the little blue car, but he didn't fit; he was a corpulent man. He heard a door slam, or thought he did... Panic disconcerted him for a moment, and then he was running across the open ground, in every direction, coming down the mountain to the plain, while dawn was breaking, at an impossibly early hour.

16

SILVIA BALERO, WHO unbeknownst to the gamblers carried a child in her belly (if they'd known, they would have bet him too), was left in the legal possession of Chiquito, although unaware of it herself, being profoundly asleep. At some point in the night the faucets in the bathroom of her hotel room opened automatically, and the tub began to fill with boiling red water, which spun and eddied and gave off steam that was also red, boiling, and sulphurous.

When Chiquito rose from the gambling table, at which he had been the only winner, and made a tour of the hotel (which had also become his property) with lurching steps—not because of the drinking, which never affected him, or the many hours of immobility, which his profession had already accustomed him to, but purely for the pleasure of lurching, for the brutish coquetry of it. It was all his; and to this he was also accustomed, because he always won. He was the luckiest gambler in the universe, and a legend had been woven around him, a legend and a great enigma—what did he keep working for? For years the gamblers of Pringles had had their sights fixed on him, each of them proposing, on his own, to beat him at a game of cards; they knew that only one would manage it, only once, and that event, if it came, would be a great triumph over luck. He didn't know this, and it wouldn't have worried him in the least if he had. On the contrary, he would have laughed his head off.

He crossed the dark lobby, looking around with cloudy eyes. It was all his, as it had been so many times, as always. And there was nothing that wasn't his, because there were no travelers checked in ... Wait a minute: yes, there was someone, a beautiful stranger ... who was also his, because he'd won her from the masked man. He set off looking for her, without stumbling. He opened the doors of all the rooms, all of them empty, until finally he came upon Silvia Balero's. She was deeply asleep in the midst of a reddish fog. He stood looking at her for a moment ... Then he went to the bathroom, and stood looking at the red water boiling in the tub. Finally he stripped and submerged himself. No one could have withstood that temperature, but it did nothing to him. His heart nearly stopped beating, his eyes closed halfway, and his mouth opened in a stupid grimace.

The next step was to violate the sleeping woman. He didn't notice she was pregnant; he thought she was only big-bellied, like so many women in the south of Argentina. Consequently, inside, a few pale blue little fingers grasped his member like a handle, and when he withdrew, puzzled, he dragged out a hairy phosphorescent fetus, ugly and deformed like a demon, who woke Silvia Balero with its shrieking and obliged them both to flee, leaving it master of the scene.

That was how the Monster came into the world.

17

IDLE DAYS IN Patagonia . . .

Tourist days in Paris . . .

Life carries people to all kinds of distant places, and generally takes them to the most far flung, to the extremes, since there's no reason to slow its momentum before it's done. Further, always further . . . until there is no further anymore, and men rebound, and lie exposed to a climate, to a light . . . A memory is a luminous miniature, like the hologram of the princess, in that movie, that the faithful robot carried in his circuits from galaxy to galaxy. The sadness inherent in any memory comes from the fact that its object is forgetting. All movement, the great horizon, the journey, is a spasm of forgetting, which bends in the bubble of memory. Memory is always portable, it is always in the hands of a wandering automaton.

The world, life, love, work: winds. Great crystalline trains that whistle through the sky. The world is wrapped in winds that come and go ... But it's not so simple, so symmetrical. The actual winds, the air masses displaced between differences in pressure, always go toward the same place in the end, and they come together in the Argentinian skies; big winds and little winds, the cosmopolitan oceanic winds as much as the diminutive backyard breezes: a funnel of stars gathers them all together, adorned with their velocities and orientations like ribbons in their hair, and brings them to rest in that privileged region of the atmosphere called Patagonia. That's why the clouds there are ephemera par excellence, as Leibniz said of objects ("objects are momentary minds": a chair is exactly like a man who lives for a single instant). The Patagonian clouds welcome and accommodate all transformations within a single instant, every transformation without exception. That's why the instant, which in any other place is as dry and fixed as a *click*, is fluid and mysterious in Patagonia, fantastic. Darwin called it: Evolution. Hudson: Attention.

I'm not talking in patriotic metaphors. This is real.

Traveling is real. Opening the door to all fears is real, even if what comes before and what comes after, the motives and the consequences, are not. To tell the truth I can't figure out how it is that people can make the decision to travel. Maybe it would be helpful to study the work of those Japanese poets who trekked from landscape to landscape finding subjects for their somewhat incoherent compositions. Maybe the explanation lies there. "The next morning the sky was very clear, and just when the sun shone brightest, we rowed out into the bay." (Bashō)

The skies of Patagonia are always clean. The winds meet there for a great carnival of invisible transformations. It's as if to say that everything happens there, and the rest of the world dissolves in the distance, useless—China, Poland, Egypt... Paris, the luminous miniature. Everything. All that remains is that radiant space, Argentina, beautiful as paradise.

How to travel? How to live in another place? Wouldn't it be lunacy, self-annihilation? To not be Argentinian is to drop into nothingness, and no one likes that.

And in full transparency... I want to make note of an idea, although it has nothing to do with all this, before I forget: might it be that the Chinese ideograms were originally conceived to be written on glass, so they could be read from the other side? Maybe that's the source of the whole misunderstanding.

And in full transparency, I was saying... a wedding dress. A cloud? No. A white dress, without the form of a dress, of course, or rather: without the form of a human, which it takes when placed on its owner or a mannequin, but instead its authentic form, the pure form of a dress, which no one ever has occasion to see, because it's not simply a question of seeing it as a mountain of fabric thrown over a table or chair. That is formlessness. The form of a dress is a continuous transformation, limitless.

And it was the most beautiful and complicated wedding dress ever made, an unfolding of all the white folds, a soft model of a universe of whites. Flying at thirty thousand feet with what appeared to be majestic slowness, even though it must have been going very fast (there was no point of reference in the blue abyss of daylight), and changing shape ceaselessly, endlessly, giant swan, forever opening new wings, its tail forty-two feet long, hyperfoam, exquisite corpse, flag of my country.

18

SO MANY YEARS have passed that by now it must be Tuesday!

.....

I'd left Delia wandering in the desolate twilight. After several hours of uncertain walking, she began to wonder where she would spend the night. She felt lost, suspended in an inhuman fatigue. A little more, very little, and she would be walking like an automaton, a lunatic. And now it didn't really matter which way she went; if there was any apparition, anywhere, she'd go toward it. What alarmed her was the feeling that she was at the extreme end of caring: when she came out on the other side she would not change direction again. The night could, at a whim, become the kind of uniform desert that would invade her soul, and that possibility filled her with terror. A house, a roof, a cave, a cabin!

An abandoned ranch, a shack, a shed! She knew that even from the depths of fatigue she could find the will to make any room habitable for a night, even the most deplorable ... She saw herself sweeping it, putting it in order, making the bed, washing the curtains ... They were absurd fantasies, but they consoled her a little even as her sense of abandonment grew, the plateau stretching out more and more and the horizon unfolding a new fringe of white, and another—did it make any sense to keep going?

It was practically nighttime. The only thing left was for darkness to fall. Each moment seemed like the last chance to glimpse a sign of salvation. And in one moment, finally, she saw something: two long, low parallelograms resting far in the distance, like two hyphens. She went toward them on winged feet, feeling all the pain of fatigue coiling in her veins. It was then that darkness fell (it must have been midnight) and the sky filled with stars.

She could no longer see her object, but still, she saw it. She hurried. She didn't care if she was running toward her downfall. There were so many downfalls! She'd never been lost in the dark before, rushing toward the first shape she saw in the last light to beg for refuge and consolation ... but there's a first time for everything. Nothing else mattered to her.

Delia was a young woman; she was barely past thirty. She was small, strong, well formed. It's not a mere literary device to only say it now. For us children (I was her eleven-year-old son's best friend), she was a señora, one of the mothers, an ugly and threatening old lady ... But there were other perspectives. It is the child's point of view that makes women look ridiculous; more precisely, it makes them look like transvestites, and therefore somewhat comical, like social artifacts whose only purpose, once the child's perspective is pushed aside a little, is to make us laugh. And even so, they are real women, sexual, desirable, beautiful ... Delia was one. Now, writing this, I ought to perform the readjustment, and it's not easy. It's as if my whole life were exhausted by the effort, and there remained no man with pen in hand, only a ghost ... Now as I say "Delia was one" I am falsifying things, making ghosts of them. No, Delia is not the luminous miniature in the reels of any movie projector. I said she was a real woman, and I submit myself to my words, to some of them at least ... to the words before they make sentences, when they are still purely present.

Suddenly she saw the enormous rectangles rise before her, like black walls that mercifully blocked her way. For most of the last three hundred feet she had believed that they were walls, but on arriving she saw her mistake: it was a truck, one of those gigantic tractor trailers, like the one that parked on her block, Chiquito's truck ... She was so distraught it didn't occur to her even for a moment that it might be the same one (as it actually was), which would have ended her search ...

Its lights were off, it was dark and silent, like a natural formation emerging from the plateau. Its thirty wheels, as tall as Delia, inflated with pounds of black pressure, rested on perfectly level earth. That's what must have given it the appearance of a building.

The castaway marched toward the front of the truck, and on coming to the cabin she went carefully around, walking on tiptoe to see inside. The windshield, the size of a movie screen, covered the upper half of the truck's flat front end. The constellations were reflected in the glass, and there was also a collection of butterflies smashed across it that the driver had not taken the trouble to clean off. The little pieces of wing, pale blue, orange, yellow, all with a metallic brilliance that intensified the light from the sky—were stuck there by their phosphorescent gel, tracing out capricious shapes in which Delia, even in her distraction, recognized lambs, tiny cars, trees, profiles, even butterflies.

Inside she saw no one, but that didn't surprise her. She knew that truck drivers, when they parked for the night to sleep, went to bed in a little compartment behind the cabin, sometimes with room for two people or more. People said they were pretty comfortably arranged. She'd never seen one, but she'd heard about them. Omar, her son, had told her about the personal comforts Chiquito had in his truck, which we were always climbing on when we played. Even after making the appropriate deprecations for fantasy and the relative dimensions of a child, she'd believed him, because others had confirmed it and it was reasonable anyway. She was sure this nocturnal truck, so large and modern, would be no smaller than the one in her neighborhood (she didn't know it was the same one).

She went to the driver's side door and knocked. She waited a moment, and as there was no response, she knocked again. She waited. Nothing. She knocked again. Toc toc. No one answered. The truck driver did not awake. But... what a smell of fried eggs! Delia had not had a bite to eat in an enormous number of hours, so that more than surprising her, she was beside herself with indignation that that incongruous smell taunted her so impishly, and it roused her to knock on the door again. "I'm going in," she said to herself, as the silence persisted. Even so, she waited a little, and knocked again. It was useless. She knocked once more, now without much hope, and stood there for another moment, intent and expectant. She caught the smell again. It seemed obvious that it was coming from inside the truck; the truck driver must have been making dinner. And with her outside, dead from hunger and exhaustion, hundreds of miles from home! "I'm going in there, I don't care," she thought, but a remaining scrap of courtesy made her knock again, three times with her knuckles on the solid metal of the door, which felt like iron. She waited to see if he happened to hear her this time, but he didn't.

Getting in, once the decision was made, was not so easy. Those trucks seemed to be made for giants. The door was extremely high. But it had a kind of foothold and from there she managed to reach the handle. It wasn't locked, but activating the hydraulic door handle demanded almost superhuman strength. In the end she managed it by hanging from it with all her weight. The door of a truck, like any vehicle, inverse to that of a house, opens out. And this one opened all the way, welcoming her, but also carrying her along on its arc ... The foothold disappeared from beneath her feet and she was left swinging there, hanging from the handle, six feet off the ground. She couldn't believe she was pirouetting like this, like a naughty child. "And now what do I do?" she wondered with alarm. There did not appear to be a solution. She could let herself fall, trusting that she wouldn't break a leg, and then climb up again by the foothold, in which case she didn't see how she would be able to shut the door again, although that was the least of her problems. In any case, she did it the hard way: she stretched out a leg and pushed off hard from the wall of the cab, so the door began to swing shut; and then before it could make contact, at just the right moment, she let go of the handle and grabbed the side mirror. Hanging there she managed to get her body far enough into the opening to place a foot inside, and with a second act of risky acrobatics she let go of the door handle for good and got hold of the steering wheel. This was not as firm as her previous supports; it turned, and Delia, surprised, was suddenly horizontal, and in the rush of falling she opened both hands and brought them to her face. Luckily she fell inside, on the floor of the cab, but with her head hanging out, and the door, on its last swing, was coming toward her ... It would have neatly decapitated her if an unknown force hadn't stopped it a millimeter from her neck. The sharp metal edge retreated softly and Delia, without waiting for it to come back, pulled her head out of the way. She moved around, extremely uncomfortable, trying to get onto the seat. The space was so large, or she was so small, that she was able to stand up, with her back to the windshield.

She tried to turn halfway around to sit and wait for her heart to calm down, but she couldn't. With terror she felt a steely pressure that circled her waist and kept her from moving. If she had fainted—and it wouldn't have taken much more of that paralyzing fear to make her do it—she would have stayed on her feet, held up by the pitiless ring. And it wasn't an illusion, or a cramp; she put both hands on her waist and felt a kind of rigid snake, hard and smooth to the touch, circling her like an impious belt. She tried to scream, but no sound came from her open mouth. She could turn right and left, but always in the same spot—the thing didn't give even an inch, although curiously it allowed itself to make a quarter-turn with her every time she tried it. It took her several agonizing seconds to understand that when she'd gotten to her feet she'd put her body through the steering wheel, which now had her by the waist.

She clambered up out of it and let herself fall on the seat, which smelled like leather and grease, and curled up panting, wondering for the thousandth time why such disagreeable things had to happen to her. She was so worn out she might have fallen asleep if it hadn't been for the frying smell, which was, she noticed only now, even more intense inside the truck.

It took her a moment to calm down and reconsider her situation. She'd landed facing the windshield, and what she saw through it made her raise her head. Before her lay marvelous nighttime Patagonia, whole and limitless. It was a plateau as white as the moon, under a black sky filled with stars. Too big, too beautiful, to be taken in with a single gaze; and yet it must be, because no one has two gazes. The panorama appeared to repose against the pure black of the night, and at the same time it was pure light. It was scored with little black marks, like holes in space, that traced out sharp, capricious shapes, in which chance seemed to have been the determining factor in representing all of the things a fluctuating consciousness might want to recognize, but without recognizing them completely, as if the plethora of figures exceeded the existence of objects. Those marks were the reverse side of the pieces of butterfly wing stuck to the glass of the windshield.

When Delia could finally take her eyes off this splendid spectacle, she admired the instruments that adorned the dashboard. There were hundreds of gauges, little clocks, needles, switches, dials, buttons ... Would a person need all that to drive a truck? There wasn't one gear shift: there were three, and ten more bristled from the crossbar of the steering wheel. The wheel itself was so enormous it didn't seem strange that she'd gotten stuck in it by accident; it would have been strange if she'd missed it. Underneath, in the shadows, she could make out a jumble of pedals. She felt very small, very diminished; she remembered to take her feet off the seat.

But then she had to put them on it again, and even worse, stand on it, to reach the trucker's compartments. She knew from Omar's descriptions that the entrance was above the headrest, and she leaned in to look. A double horizontal partition, which cut twice across a golden light. She thought of calling out, but some faint noises and the muffled echo of a voice made her suddenly afraid. The truth was she didn't know what she had gotten herself into, what lion's den. But it was no longer a question of retreat. With the ever-flawed logic of polite intruders, she preferred not to call out but to enter on tiptoe instead, to temper the surprise a bit; she didn't want to give the unprepared trucker a heart attack, or fail to give him time to put on his pants.

She climbed in, legs first. When she let go she fell further than expected. She slid down one of the screens, which was on an incline, being attached by hinges to the back wall of the cab. In this highway bedroom she could now see what she had heard so much about. There were two beds very close together, both unmade. The disorder and filth were indescribable: comic books, clothes, dissected birds, knives, shoes ... A lit candle on the bureau illuminated the little room. For a lost woman, alone, like Delia was, such an atmosphere could have presaged anything.

Part of her consciousness knew that, and another part was occupied with trying to see what would happen next, and that part took the initiative: she went through one of the two doors at random, crossed a room full of junk she didn't look at and went through another door, into a small room with leather armchairs. She stopped there, looking at them in disbelief. There was no light here except what came through an open door, through which she could hear noises. The room had four doors, one on each side. They were all open. She glanced into the darkest one, which led to a hallway, and then the next: an office, with a great roll-top desk, where the disorder and filth of the bedroom were repeated. She crossed the room and went out through the door on the other side, where she found herself in a vestibule with chairs. And three doors. She went through the first on the left: an unoccupied bedroom, with the bed made. Actually it seemed less like a bed than a kind of low, elastic table ... There, also, was another door. She noticed, in retrospect, that it was the same in all the rooms, as if someone had been preoccupied with achieving maximum circulation. The result was that she was lost. She went on, and came somehow to the kitchen, which was the source of the light that spread throughout the whole labyrinth.

Here she thought the moment of truth had come, but there was nobody there. The burner was lit however, and two frying eggs crackled in the pan. The cook must have gone out for a moment, maybe in search of her, if he'd heard her. A large Petromax lantern cast a blinding light through the bastion of containers and foodstuffs. The pile of dirty dishes was incredible, and there were scraps thrown everywhere, even stuck to the walls and ceiling. A summary glance at the pan indicated that the eggs were almost perfect. On the counter, half a bottle of red wine and a glass. She lost her nerve and hurried out: she burst into the room she'd been in before, which seemed different to her now, as a new odor redoubled her trembling. Following a spiral of smoke with her eyes, she saw that in the ashtray on the end table was a recently lit Brasil cigarette. But there was still no one there ... How strange.

Delia's aversion to tobacco smoke was extreme and fairly inexplicable. She couldn't conceive of smoking inside a house. She had managed to get her husband to give up the habit when they married, a minor but nonetheless remarkable miracle. To a certain extent, she'd forgotten about it. She stood watching with incredulous horror as the smoke rose in the supernatural stillness of the room.

Chiquito came in through the door from the hallway and leaned down to pick up the cigarette. He was in boxer shorts and an undershirt, hairy, unkempt, and with the face of a man who had few friends. He went into the kitchen.

He came back almost immediately with the fried eggs in the pan. He crossed the room and exited through the same door he'd come from before ... At the end of the hall there was a dining room. Delia, peering out from behind the chair where she'd hidden, saw him sit down at the table, empty the frying pan over the plate and settle down to eat. She recognized him, and the surprise paralyzed her. In an instant, and without being any kind of intellectual, she was suddenly inspired to summarize the situation in an epigrammatic inversion of what she'd been saying up until now: in fact it was she, Delia herself, without meaning to, who had played a dirty trick on her own destiny.

Suddenly Chiquito let out a yelp. He'd put a whole egg in his mouth without remembering to take the cigarette out from between his lips, and the ember had burned his tongue. He spat out a jet of viscous yellow and white stuff, splattering a woman seated across from him. It was Silvia Balero, who had undergone a pronounced transformation since her last fitting with the seamstress: she was black. Down her black face, chest and arms ran the egg slobber, but she didn't move a muscle. She looked like an ebony statue. Chiquito ran out groaning into the hallway and came back with a band-aid on his tongue. He drank several glasses of wine in a row. Miss Balero remained immobile, unblinking, and completely covered in that bruised black color. The truck driver finished his dinner, peeled an orange and threw the skin carelessly on the floor, and finally lit another cigarette. Through all of this he'd been talking to his guest, but with guttural, incomprehensible words. The black woman shook herself at intervals and let out some senseless phrases. It was incredible that a natural blonde with such a white complexion had taken on that dark veneer overnight. Chiquito, his accident already forgotten, was roaring with laughter; he seemed happy, not a care in the world...

Until he lit his third or fourth after-dinner Brasil cigarette and Delia, behind the armchair, couldn't help a sigh or little cough of irritation (the air was becoming unbreathable): Chiquito heard her and turned his formidable bulk in a violent twist that made his chair creak as the legs scraped together. How strange that someone so solid had gotten that diminutive nickname: Chiquito. Surely they'd given it to him as a child, and it had stuck. To think of antiphrasis or irony would have been out of place given his background.

Delia crawled backwards to the closest door, and as soon as she thought she was out of sight she ran. Luckily there were exits everywhere ... But that very extravagance only contributed to her running around in circles within the labyrinth, and increased the risk of running straight into the hands of her pursuer. Delia had abandoned any idea of asking for refuge or help in getting home. Not from him, at least. She hadn't had time to think, with all the surprises and fear, but it didn't matter. She was discovering that one could also think outside of time.

Chiquito was bearing down on her, shouting:

"Who's there, who's there ..."

"At least he didn't recognize me," Delia said to herself, hoping even in her desperation to preserve their coexistence within the neighborhood ... if she ever got back there.

She was looking for the bedroom she'd first come in through, to get out by way of the hanging screens ... but she came out somewhere completely different, in a dark and intricate jumble of metal. She was helplessly caught in its twists and turns. As if the inertia weren't enough, she insisted on continuing forward, sticking a leg in, and then another, an arm, her head ... It was the truck's engine, asleep for the moment ... But what if it turned on? Those iron pieces, in motion, would grind her up in a second ... She felt something sticky on her hands: it was filthy black grease that covered her from head to toe. It was the finishing touch. She could hardly move, neither backward nor forward, caught in the machinery from all sides ... And Chiquito's shouts and footsteps were getting closer, they boomed in the mastodonic pistons ... she was lost!

At that moment a great jolt shook everything. For a moment Delia feared the most horrible thing had happened: the engine was starting. But it was not that. The agitation multiplied, and the whole truck danced clumsily on its thirty wheels. A deafening whistle enveloped it and passed through the metal walls. All the smells came back to her, and then vanished. A current of cold air touched her.

"The wind has picked up," she automatically thought. And what a wind!

Chiquito's reaction was surprising. He started to scream like a lunatic. It was as if his worst enemy had appeared at the very worst moment.

"You again, damn you! You damned wind! Son of a thousand whores! This time you won't get away! I'm going to kill youuuuu!"

The wind's response was to increase its force a thousand times. The truck shuddered, its metal walls rattled, the whole inside crashed together . . . and, most importantly, it seemed to expand with the air forced in under pressure—into the engine parts too . . . Delia felt herself get free, and immediately a current of air snatched her up and carried her away, bouncing and sliding in the grease, toward a vortex in the radiator, in the grille where the whistles refracted like ten symphonic orchestras in a gigantic concert . . . The chrome grille flew off, and Delia jumped after it, and now she was outside, running like a gazelle.

19

SHE WAS SURPRISED how fast she was going, like an arrow. She often boasted, and rightly so, of her agility and energy; but that was inside the house, sweeping, washing, cooking and so on, hurrying through the neighborhood with short little steps when she went out to do her shopping, never running. Now she was running without any effort, and she was eating up the distance. The air whistled in her ears. "What speed!" she said to herself, "This is what fear can do!"

When she stopped, the whistling dropped to a whisper, but it persisted. The wind still wrapped itself around her.

"Delia ... Delia ..." a voice called, from very close by.

"Huh? Who ...? What ...? Who's calling me?" asked Delia, but she corrected her somewhat peremptory tone for fear of offending; she felt so alone, and her name sounded so exquisitely sweet. "Yes? It's me, I'm Delia. Who's calling me?" She said it almost smiling, with an expression of intrigue and interest, if a little fearful as well, because it seemed like magic. There was no one nearby, or far away either, and the truck was no longer in sight.

"It's me, Delia."

"No, I'm Delia."

"I mean: Delia, oh Delia, it's me who speaks to you."

"Who is me? Pardon me, sir, but I don't see anyone."

It was a man's voice: low, refined, modulated with a superior calm.

"Me: the wind."

"Ah. A voice carried by the wind? But where is the man?"

"There is no man. I am the wind."

"The wind talks?"

"You're hearing me."

"Yes, yes, I hear you. But I don't understand ... I didn't know the wind could talk."

"I can."

"What wind are you?"

"My name is Ventarrón."

The name sounded familiar.

"That sounds familiar ... Have we met before?"

"Many times. Let's see if you remember."

"Do you remember?"

"Of course."

She tried to think.

"It wasn't that time ... ?"

"Yes, yes."

"And that other time, when ...?"

"Yes! What a good physiognomist you are."

He wasn't joking. It must have been a figure of speech.

"So many times . . .! Now I remember others, but it would take me hours to mention them all."

"I would listen to you without ever feeling bored. It would be like music for me."

"Millions of times."

"Not so many, Delia, not so many. It's just that I'm unmistakable."

He was very friendly, really. But poor Delia was in no condition to carry her courtesy to the point of launching into Proustian record-keeping, so she moved on to a more immediate matter.

"You're the one who saved me from the truck driver?"

"Yes."

"Thank you. You don't know how much I appreciate it."

"I've been looking after you since you came here, Delia. Who did you think saved you from those rough-housing winds that were dancing you all over the sky and set you down safely on the ground? Who stopped the truck door when it was about to cut off your head?"

"It was you?"

"Yes."

"Then thank you. I didn't mean to be so much trouble."

"I did it because I liked doing it."

"I just don't know why all those accidents had to happen to me, I don't know how I got myself into all this trouble . . . All I know is that I went out looking for my son . . ."

"Things happen, Delia."

"But they've never happened to me before."

"That's true."

"And now . . . I'm lost, alone, with nothing . . ."

She whimpered a little, overwhelmed.

"I'm here. I'll make sure nothing bad happens to you."

"But you're just a wind! Excuse me, I don't know what I'm saying. It's just that I want my son, my house . . . !"

"All you have to do is say so, Delia. I can bring you whatever you want. Your house, you said?"

"No!" Delia exclaimed, already seeing her house flying through the air and falling, a pile of rubble, at her feet in that desolate place. "No . . . Let me think. You can really bring me whatever I ask for?"

"That's why I'm the wind."

She would have liked to ask him for just the opposite: to carry her back to her house . . . But, in addition to her fear of flying, she kept in mind that that was not what Ventarrón had offered her. She began to feel suspicious. The question which came to mind at that point was: "Why me?" But she didn't dare ask him. What she had heard up until now sounded like a declaration of love, and she didn't know what intentions this mysterious being could have. She preferred to keep talking along a less compromising route.

"It must be interesting being a wind."

"I'm not just any wind. I'm the fastest and the strongest. You already saw what I did to that truck."

"That was very impressive. That man was starting to scare me. You know he's a neighbor of mine, in Pringles?"

Silence.

"Of course I know."

"What I can't figure out is how Miss Balero got there."

"You'll find out . . . ."

"I hope he won't think of following me."

"He will pursue you, he'll do nothing else from this moment on."

"Really?"

"But don't worry, that's what I'm here for."

"Forgive me, sir, but I don't think a wind, no matter how strong it might be, can stop a truck."

The wind snorted with disdain.

"No one can defeat me! No one! Look how I run!" He went to the horizon and back. "Look how I stop!" He stopped on a dime. "Watch this jump!" He executed a prodigious pirouette. "Up! Down!"

The night was clear, like a dark blue day. The moon watched impassively. Delia thought she saw it, but she wasn't sure. If she hadn't been so impressed, the display would have seemed a little puerile.

Ventarrón returned to her side, and then she was sure she saw him, invisible, strong and beautiful, like a god.

"Now, what do you want?"

She still didn't know what she should ask for.

"Could I have ... something to eat?"

"Of course!"

He left and was back in a minute, bringing a table, a chair, a tablecloth, plates, silverware, a napkin, a salt shaker, a chicken-fried steak with French fries, a glass of wine and a pear with cream. It all came flying, loose, the French fries like a swarm of golden lobsters, the cream whipped up into a little cloud ... But it all settled in an orderly way on the table, and the chair was pulled out for her with the greatest courtesy ... She didn't even have to unfold the napkin and put it on her lap, because Ventarrón did it for her.

"It's only missing the candles, but I couldn't light them," he told her. "It goes against my nature. At any rate, the moon, which I've been polishing so it will shine more brightly, will be your lamp."

"Thank you very much."

He stayed off at a certain distance, whistling, until she finished. Then he pulled out the chair, Delia stood up, and he carried it all away.

"Who knows who he snatched it from," the seamstress thought. "To think I had to eat what a thieving wind brought me!"

"Now you'll want to sleep."

Just then a bed, a mattress, sheets, a fur blanket, and a pillow came flying in from the horizon. The bed was made up before her eyes in an instant, without a single wrinkle.

"Sweet dreams."

"Thank you . . ."

His voice had become caressing, as had he. He wrapped himself around her, ruffling her hair and her dress, circling her legs with velvet breaths . . .

"Until tomorrow, Delia."

"Until tomorrow, Ventarrón."

There was a kind of whirlwind of absence, and the wind climbed into the starry sky. Delia stood for a moment, unsure, beside the bed. The wine had made her very sleepy. The white knit sheets invited her to sleep. She looked around. It was a little incongruent, this bed in the middle of the plain. And her dress was impossibly greasy. She hesitated a moment, and then said to herself, lying to herself with the truth: "No one can see me." She stripped, and as she slid under the sheets her body shone in the moonlight. The night sighed.

20

WHEN SHE WOKE the next morning she thought she was at home, as often happens to travelers ... Except for her it was not a brief, fleeting state, a short lapse of incomprehension ... instead, the strangeness of it settled in her mind like a world, and stayed there. Under normal circumstances, she was in her bed, her bed was in her bedroom, her bedroom was in her house, and her house was in Pringles. Today, however, it looked like that whole chain of familiarity had been broken. The sky was very blue, and the sun was a white dot set in the most distant part of it. She turned to her right, and there was no Ramón beside her, and beyond that no child's bed, no sleeping Omar. To her left there was no dresser with its mirror on top ... and, therefore, no reflection of the window over Omar's bed ... In a word, she was not at home. She was not anywhere. An immense space surrounded her on all sides. The only thing that seemed to be in its place was the time, although not even the late dawn in that place had a particular time: one could call it a lapse in eternity. It didn't feel like time to get up ... She stretched.

Days of idleness in Patagonia ...

When she put on her dress she could see now, in the light, what a greasy disaster it was. Her shoes were impossibly covered with dust, she could have written on them with her finger. The wind, so helpful for other things, had not taken care of her clothes, probably because she hadn't asked him to. It occurred to her that he must be like those maids who are very hardworking and efficient, but lack initiative, and have to be told to do everything.

"Good morning, Delia."

"Ah, um ... Good morning."

"Did you sleep well?"

"Perfectly. I wanted ..."

"One moment. I have to take this."

The bed and everything on it flew away at full speed and was lost beyond the horizon. "Such a hurry," Delia thought. In an instant the wind was back.

"Delia, I have to tell you something I would have preferred to keep to myself, but it's better for you to know, just in case."

"About what? Don't scare me ..." Delia was already thinking of catastrophes, as was her custom.

"Last night," began Ventarrón, "I went out for a stroll, after you fell asleep, and over there I saw a light, and got closer to look. There's a hotel there, on top of a little mountain, and at first I thought it was on fire, it glowed so brightly. But there was no fire. I went down and looked in the windows. It wasn't a party either. It was a radioactive kind of light, pulsing, pulsing so much it shook the whole hotel . . . A red, horrible light, and the temperature had risen to several thousand degrees . . . As I had no intention of becoming an atomic wind, I moved back, and stayed there watching. It went from bad to worse. Even I started to become frightened, though there's no one better at getting away than me. But I know there are distant terrors from which escape is useless. And then, all at once, the whole hotel fell in, melted like a snowflake in the sun . . . And there it was—free, burning and horrible—the Monster . . . the child who should never have been born . . ."

His voice, already naturally low, had taken on a from-beyond-the-grave resonance, very pessimistic. His last words gave Delia goose bumps along her spine.

"What child . . . ? What monster . . . ?"

"There is a legend that says that one day, in a hot springs hotel in this area, a child will be born who is gifted with all the power of transformation, a being that will encapsulate all of the winds in the world, an über-wind, and therefore terrifyingly ugly . . . At least for me, and for you, because what in me is exterior, in him is interior, fostering all kinds of deformations . . . Now you see why it impressed me so."

"And what happened?"

"Nothing. I ran away, and here I am. The problem is that the Monster is loose, and he's looking for you."

"For me?! Why me?"

"Because that's what the legend says," answered the wind, cryptically. "And it's obvious that the legend has come true."

"But where could this Monster have come from?"

"Evolution follows no path."

"And the truck driver is looking for me too, no?"

"I'll take care of the truck driver, he's not a problem."

"And the Monster?"

Silence.

"That's something else," said Ventarrón.

Delia lowered her head, overwhelmed.

"Changing the subject," said the wind. "Last night I saw another thing which enchanted me: a great wedding dress, folding and unfolding at thirty thousand feet up, sailing south ..."

"A wedding dress? With nylon voile cuffs, satin ...?"

"Yes! But what do I know about fabrics! Why do you ask?"

"Because it's mine. I lost it yesterday, or the day before yesterday ..."

"Yours how? Aren't you married? Didn't you tell me you had a son?"

"No. I mean I was sewing it, for a girl who just ..."

"Don't tell me you're a seamstress?!"

"Yes."

The wind almost fell over. He took a while to recover.

"You're the seamstress then? Ramón Siffoni's wife?"

"Yes. I thought you knew that."

"Now I'm starting to understand. It's all beginning to line up. The seamstress ... and the wind."

"The two of us."

"The two of us ..."

The wind was in love. He'd been in love for all eternity, or at least for all of his wind-eternity. And now that the story was starting to unfold before him, he found it suddenly too real, shrill, paradoxically unpredictable ...

"Sir . . ." Delia interrupted his meditation.

"Yes?"

"You told me you could bring me what I asked you for?"

". . ."

"Would you bring me the dress?"

"What do you want it for?"

Yes, well put, what for? It didn't look like Miss Balero, who was now black and in the power of that savage truck driver, was going to need it. But one never knew; in any case, she could charge for the labor and turn it over to Miss Balero's mother; it was already practically done. Besides, it was reasonable to ask for it, since it was her work.

"The customer provided the fabric," she said, "and she's going to want it back."

"All right, but give me time. Who knows where it might be by now."

"One more little thing, if it's not too much trouble. I brought a sewing kit, and I lost it, surely the things are spread all over . . . Could you gather them up and bring me the box?"

"Don't worry about it. I'm very good at finding lost needles in Patagonia."

"What I don't know is what to do in the meantime."

"I never get bored," said the wind.

"Neither do I, when I'm at home. But here . . ." she whimpered again.

"I already told you I can bring you your house, with everything in it."

"No, no . . . I don't want it!"

She could think of nothing more depressing than her house

set there in the middle of the desert; for her the house was the street too, the neighbors, the neighborhood. Offering her the house by itself was like trying to pay her with an inconceivable one-sided coin.

"We'd be very comfortable, Delia, you here in your house, cleaning, cooking, sewing. I would keep you company, bring you everything you wanted ... we would live happily, safely ..."

Delia was terrified. Ventarrón's intentions were becoming clear, and they filled her with dread. Was it possible that a meteorological phenomenon had fallen in love with her? And besides, he was contradicting himself: how was she going to be safe? There was an insane truck driver, and on top of that a monster out to destroy her! It was not a very soothing perspective. And there were her husband and son. She didn't want to talk about that with the wind, but he brought the subject up.

"Would you like your husband to come get you?"

"..."

"He won't be able to, Delia. He tried, but his vice intervened (you already know what I'm talking about), and he lost the truck."

"Really?"

"And he won't be able to get it back. That little red truck you were so accustomed to is now invisible, and no one will ever drive it again. Ramón Siffoni has been left on his feet forever."

I will never return to Pringles! thought Delia with desperation. She hated the wind for his sadism.

"I have to ask you something, Delia. Are you in love with your husband? Did you marry for love?"

"And why else would I get married?"

"To keep from ending up an old maid."

She didn't deign to respond. She might not have been able to even if she'd wanted, because she had a knot in her throat.

"Do you love him?"

"Yes."

"But you've never told him so."

"It's not necessary in marriage."

"How unromantic you are!" A pause. "Do you want to tell him?"

In a fit, Delia forgot her prudence.

"If only he were here I'd tell him! If only!"

"He doesn't have to be here. I could carry your words to the other side of the world, if necessary." Another pause. The wind waited. "Tell him. Be brave and tell him."

Delia raised her head and looked at the horizon, out there at the end of the plateau. It all seemed very small, and yet she knew it was very big. Could her voice cross it? Her voice was in her husband's heart ... How big the world was! And how far away she was! Where had she come to rest? She would never go back to Pringles! Never!

"Ramón ... " she said, and the wind roared and was gone.

21

I'M SITTING IN a café on the Place de Clichy . . . At this point I remain here against my will. I should have left a while ago, I have a commitment . . . But I can't call the waiter, I simply can't do it, it's stronger than I am, and the minutes are passing . . . I've reviewed the bill and my pocket several times, I've counted the coins from back to front and front to back and I come up short by a hair, I have six francs and ninety centimes and the coffee costs seven, it's as if it were done on purpose . . . That's why I need the waiter to come, he's going to have to give me change for fifty francs, I don't have anything smaller . . . If I had enough coins I would leave them on the table, free as a bird I would leave these little metal eggs and fly away. My impatience is so great that if I had a ten franc note I would leave it . . . But I don't. I'm reduced to waiting for him to look at me so I can make some gesture, wave him over . . . it's the same here as everywhere in the world: waiters never look your way. My eyes are fixed on him, every turn he makes I try out my gesture ... By now all the customers must have noticed, and the other waiters, of course, all except him. Let's see ... He's coming this way ... no, again I failed, I must have the air of a supplicant, I'm stuck to my chair ... I move it, I scrape the legs against the floor, to make him look at me ... I know going after him would be useless as well as grotesque, he'd slip away ... Then, I would become the invisible man, yes, the ghost of the Place de Clichy. There's nothing to do but wait for the next opportunity, hope that he turns this way, that he clears the table next to mine and sees me ... And I want to go, I have to go, that's the worst ... I've been here for two hours writing at this table (he must think that if I stayed two hours, I could just as well stay three, or five, or until they close), and in the enthusiasm of inspiration, which I'm cursing now, I went on and on until I'd finished the previous chapter ... and when I looked at the clock I wanted to die ... I should already be at that dinner, they'll be waiting for me—for me, stuck here ... I have twenty minutes on the Métro at least, and the minutes pass and I keep searching for the waiter's gaze ... I don't know how I can be writing this, if I'm not taking my eyes off his head .... Every time I put in an ellipse I make holes in the notebook. This is beginning to look definitive: he's never going to look at me, ever. Have I been trying for ten minutes? Fifteen? I don't want to look at the clock any more. I stare at him like a maniac ... The law of probabilities should be in my favor, at some point he should look at me, since he can't help looking at something ... And to think it would have been so easy to make him come over as soon as I saw the time: calling him would have been enough. So many people do it ... But I can't. Never in my life have I called a waiter except by mute craft (and I have written all my novels in cafés), I've never done it, I will never do it ... never ... And then an ardent recrimination of my Creator rises in me—mute of course, internal, though I pronounce and hear it with the greatest clarity:

"Lord, what did You give me a voice for if it's no use to me? Along with my voice, shouldn't You have given me the capacity to use it? How hard would that have been? Don't You think it's sarcastic, almost sadistic, to make me the owner of this marvelous instrument that passes from the immobile body through the air like a messenger and which is the body in another form, the body in flight ... and wrap that voice up in me, under a spell of interiority? It's as if I'm carrying a corpse inside, or at least an invalid, or a guest who won't leave ... I suppose as a newborn I could scream to call my mother like anybody else ... but then what? My voice has atrophied in my throat, and when I speak—and I only speak when spoken to, like a ghost—what comes out is an adenoidal and affected stammer barely adequate for carrying my ignorance and doubts across very short distances. If You'd at least made me mute, I'd be calmer! Then I could yell, and I'd yell all the time, the sky would be full of my dumb howling! You'll say I've abused my reading of Leibniz, Lord, but don't You think, given the circumstances, You should move the waiter's head in such a way that he might see me?"

Delia, my reality ... Talking to you now, in my silence, does your story not resemble mine? It's the same, it matches in each iridescent turn ... What in me is a miniscule incident, in you becomes destiny, adventure ... And yet the two things are not dissimilar; rather, one is a rearrangement of the other. It's not the volume of the voice that matters, but its placement in the story where it's spoken; a story has corners and folds, proximities and distances . . . A word in time can do everything . . . And more than anything else (but it's all the same) what matters is what's said, the meaning; in the arrangement of the story there is a silver bridge, a continuum, from voice to meaning, from the body to the soul, and the story advances by that continuum, by that bridge . . .

I left off just at the release of the voice . . . The wind left with the words of love riding on his back, and crossed vast distances in all directions. To throw them off he shook, he twisted, but he managed only to turn the words around, point them elsewhere, drive them into the interstices of Patagonia. The wind too had a lot to learn. In his life there was only one restriction on total freedom: the Coriolis effect, the force of gravity applied to his mass—which is just what keeps all winds stuck to the planet. The voice, for its part, has the peculiarity that when released it carries the weight of the body from which it has come; since that weight is erotic reality, lovers believe they can embrace words of love, they believe they can make them into a continuum of love that will last forever.

The continuum, by another name: the confession. If I wrote confessional literature, I would dedicate myself to seeking out the unspoken. But I don't know if I would find it; I don't know if the unspoken exists within my life. The unspoken, like love, is a thing that occupies a place in a story. Leaving aside the distances involved, it's like God. God can be placed in two different locations within a discourse: at the end, as Leibniz does when he says "and it is this that we call God"—which is to say, when one arrives at Him after the deduction of the world; or at the beginning: "God created ..." They are not different theologies, they are the same, only exposed from the other side. The kind of discourse that places God at the beginning is the model and mother of what we call "fiction." I must not forget that before my trip I proposed to write a novel. "The wind said ..." is not so absurd; it's only a method, like any other. It's a beginning. But it's always a beginning, at every moment, from the first to the last.

Words of love ... Traveling words, words that alight and stay forever balanced on the scales within the heart of a man. In Ramón and Delia's past there was a small, secret puzzle (but life is full of puzzles that are never solved). They had consummated their marriage some time after the wedding, apparently due to Ramón's desire or lack of it, although he never explained himself. What I mean to say is, there was a blank spot between the wedding and the consummation. Even if anyone besides the two of them had known about this blank spot, it would have been pointless to ask Delia about it, just as it was pointless for Delia to ask herself, because she wouldn't have known how to answer. And, that was what I was referring to, in large part, when I talked about forgetting, and memory, et cetera: there are things that seem like secrets someone is keeping, but aren't being kept by anyone.

The backbiting of neighbors, that passionate hobby at which Delia was an expert, was a similar thing. If I entered Delia's consciousness the way an omniscient narrator could, I would discover with surprise and perhaps a certain disillusionment that backbiting does not exist in her intimate heart. But it was Delia herself who was surprised! And she discovered her surprise as her own omniscient narrator ...

22

RAMÓN, MEANWHILE . . . that is to say, the day before: let's not forget that Delia had lost a day . . . was walking, lost, on the hyperflat plateau, disoriented and in a bad mood. And with good reason. He was on foot, in an endless desert . . . For a Pringlense at that time, being on foot was serious: the town was the size of a handkerchief, but for some reason, maybe precisely because it was so small, getting around on foot was no good. Everyone was motorized, the poor in ancient vehicles—the kind that ran on miracles, but were fixed up to come and go all the time, though if they didn't go, they didn't come. My grandmother used to say, "They even drive to the latrine." It was those trips which agreeably annoyed mechanics who thought they could conquer time and space. Ramón, being a gambler, went further than the others in this subjective system. In his case it was more important, more exciting: each change of place had its own importance. He wasn't the only one to dabble in these illusions, of course: he wasn't the only compulsive gambler in Pringles, not by a long shot; there was a whole constellation of them, a hierarchy of equals. As a popular joke had it, they were the ones who kept playing even when they left the green table at dawn; the sun rose so they could keep playing without knowing it; the truth was, they carried their addiction everywhere they went, in their cars or their vans, even out of town, into the surrounding country. The games were constellations, a conjunction of values telling their secrets to each other at a distance, each addictive game at its point in the black sky of the gambler's night; so they couldn't help but carry their addictions with them everywhere. It was a way of life with them: circulating at full speed, in an almost exultant simultaneity of numbers and figures.

Ramón Siffoni's quarrel with Chiquito had grown over time, as quarrels do in small towns. It had begun at some moment or other, and almost immediately had encompassed the whole of one of those private universes ... Ramón believed, not without naïveté, that it would be possible to keep the quarrel in a stable state until he decided ... what? Impossible to say. Until he decided to look his delusion in the face; a delusion is, by definition, that which always turns its back.

And now, vehicle-less, walking in a place with no roads and no way to find them, he discovered that the moment had arrived. All moments arrive, and this one too. Chiquito had taken control of everything ... of what? Of his wife? He would never have gambled Delia away at cards, he wasn't a monster, and he had other things to wager first, many other things, almost an infinite number of things ... But there was a moment, that moment, when it arrived ... in which Ramón realized the bet might have been placed anyway, without him knowing it; that had happened to him before. He'd predicted this would happen ... but now he didn't know if it had happened or not.

He walked all morning, at random, trying to keep in a straight line so he could cover more terrain, and above all so he wouldn't end up back at the hotel he'd fled. And although there's nothing in the desert, he found some surprising things. The first was the remains of a black Chrysler, smashed up and lying there. He stopped and looked it over for a while. There were no bodies inside, and it didn't look like anyone had died in the accident; he saw no blood, at least, and the whole front seat had stayed more or less intact, basketed. It was a taxi: it had a meter ... And the license plate was from Pringles. In fact, it bore an uncanny resemblance to the car that belonged to his friend Zaralegui, the taxi driver. Ramón understood a fair amount about mechanics, it was one of the many skills a life of idleness had taught him; but getting this wreck running again was out of the question, its body had been twisted so badly there was no longer any front or back. He calculated that the crash had happened at a formidable speed, there was no other way to explain how smashed up it was. The fact that such an old car had reached such a speed was a credit to the engine, an old one so perfect and solid that it had been left mostly intact; if anyone had been interested, it would have been the only recoverable thing in the wreck.

He mentally took its coordinates; he didn't know why (he couldn't even take shelter there if it rained, since the roof was now below the blown-out tires). But at least it was a thing, a discovery, something he could return to. He went on.

The second find was half-buried. It looked like a round-topped wardrobe, but on closer examination he saw that it was the magnificent shell of a gigantic Paleozoic armadillo. What stuck out was barely a fraction of it, but he discovered that the earth trapping it was fragile, crystallized, and would shatter and disperse at a breath. He dug with a loose rib, out of pure curiosity, until the whole shell lay exposed; it was twenty-four feet long, fifteen wide, and nine high at the middle. In life this had been an armadillo the size, more or less, of a baby whale. The shell was perfect, unbroken, a color you might call brown mother-of-pearl, worked over to the last quarter-inch with knots, borders, Islamic flourishes ... When it was struck it made a dry little noise, like wood. It wasn't just the upper convex part that was intact, but the lower part too, which was a thick, flat, white membrane. He moved the enormous structure to one side of the excavation and was surprised at how light it was. He crawled inside. This, yes, could serve as shelter; and it was spacious and bare. He could stand up inside it, and walk ... with some armchairs and a coffee table it would be a cozy little room. He cleaned it, tossed out what was left of the bones through the openings (there were six: one in front and one behind, for the head and tail, and four below, for the legs) and sat inside admiring the ancient marvel. The mother-of-pearl shell was not entirely opaque; it let in a very warm, very golden light. He remembered that the tails of that type of animal were also armored, and was surprised that there was nothing hanging from the back opening. Maybe it had fallen off ... He got out and looked around. He had to dig a little more, but he found it: a kind of horn of the same material, an elongated cone some eighteen or twenty feet in length, curving to a very sharp point. It was empty too, and light enough so he could stand it up, with the point on top, and shake the dirt and pebbles out.

He'd been working for hours, and was covered in sweat. He crawled in again and stretched out on the membrane, as if on a prehistoric white rug, to rest and think. An idea occurred to him; it seemed crazy, but maybe it wasn't. If he took this fossil as a chassis ... and put the Chrysler engine in it, and attached the wheels ... He was drowsy with mechanical dreams. But how would he get the engine and the other parts he needed here? He wouldn't have to bring them, he could take the shell to where they were ... He got out to try. Indeed, he could move it, but very slowly, with much difficulty, and it would take days to make the one or two miles that separated him from the car. It was a little like gambling: sometimes you have everything you need for a winning hand, but not all together ... Another idea occurred to him (which isn't so impressive: in general when an idea occurs to a person, another one occurs to him afterwards, so much so that I've come to wonder sometimes if ideas don't come to me only to provoke the occurrence of other ideas). He walked off in the direction of the Chrysler. He would have to find it again, of course, but he was confident that he could, and he did. What he'd thought of was to take the rims off the wheels, get the axles out, and make a kind of wheelbarrow to carry the engine to the shell. But it turned out that it wasn't so easy. The lack of tools didn't help, although he found a providential screwdriver in the taxi's crushed glove compartment. In the end he got the four wheels off (the circle had not been deformed on any of the four); to make the kind of wheelbarrow he'd thought of was crazy. It would be more practical to work backwards. He made four trips to the excavation site, carrying one wheel each time, another trip to bring the axles, and with the help of the obliging screwdriver he managed to attach them, precariously, to the underside of the armadillo. He pushed it, and it moved forward with perfect ease. He put the tail inside, in case it might be useful; he thought he might have to put it back in its place to act as a rudder, its natural function.

It didn't take long to pull it off. First he took the whole wreck apart, screw by screw. He jury-rigged it brilliantly; he put the engine in front, held it in with clamps, and put in the gas tank, the radiator, et cetera. The pulleys, the axles, the wheels in the four openings for the legs ... all set. It's easier to explain it than to do it, but in his case it was very easy nonetheless. The next step was to turn it on and try it out, which he did. The machine moved, slowly at first, and then faster.

23

NIGHT FELL AND he drove on and on, with the horn in front... because he'd put the armadillo's tail-cone on as the nose of his vehicle, that is to say he'd screwed it to the opening in front. It looked good, he thought; he'd done it only for aesthetics, not aerodynamics. What he liked most was that it entirely changed the appearance of the remains: with the horn in front it didn't look like an armadillo anymore. It made him think how easy it was to change the appearance of a thing, what seemed most inherent to its being, most eternal ... it was completely transformed by a measure as simple as changing the placement of the tail. How many things that seem different from each other, he thought, might actually be the same, with some little detail turned around!

What was impressive was the noise it made. The hoarseness of the engine resounded in the great hollow oval like thunder.

He hadn't slept the night before, and he was nodding off. So he parked (it made no difference where) and lay down on the membrane, behind the seat. He had more than enough room. He fell asleep immediately. Close to dawn, an abrupt shaking woke him. The circle of the setting moon had come to rest just inside the tail opening, which was the only entrance or exit from the vehicle. He barely managed to wonder if he'd been dreaming before a second shake, this one more prolonged, rocked him again. It kept going while he got to his feet, stiff and still half asleep. The shell was rocking back and forth so much that Ramón fell three times before he could get hold of the back of the seat. Once he was sitting down, he looked out through the half-moon he'd left open in the upper part of the hole in front, over the steering wheel, which made a windshield without glass. The plateau was dim and tranquil, and the grass wasn't moving. The vehicle kept vibrating, a little less now, and as soon as he could orient his attention he realized that the blows and scrapes were coming from above, from the cupola of the marvelous mother-of-pearl shell. Evidently some animal had climbed onto it; it wouldn't have to be very big to shake the structure like that, being so light, but it might be dangerous anyway. He decided to check with the Chrysler's rearview mirror, which he'd taken the precaution of bringing along. He grabbed it and stuck his hand out through the half-moon, pointing it backwards. What he saw froze his blood with fear.

It was the Monster. Ramón had never seen anything so ugly, but then, nobody else had ever seen anything so ugly either. It was a child monster. Perched on the roof … the way Omar always perched on Chiquito's truck … children liked to do that.

The chilling thing was the Monster's shape … More than a

shape it was an accumulation of shapes, fluid and fixed at once, fluid in space and fixed in time, and vice versa ... There was no explanation for it. The monster had seen (because it had eyes, or one eye, or it was an eye) the mirror coming out of the slot, shining in the light of the moon, and he stretched toward it ...

Ramón pulled his hand, which had begun to tremble, back inside, put in the clutch, stepped on the accelerator ... The vehicle surged forward, with the monster tumbling around on top.

Omar ... the game ... the monster child ... the lost child ... It all tumbled in his mind, like the creature on the roof of the Paleomobile ... He saw Omar duplicated in his inseparable friend César Aira ... He trusted that the Airas had taken Omar in and fed him that night and the night before; in the end, it didn't matter ... But how paradoxical, in the middle of all this, for the lost child to be at home, and the parents circling and circling in the desert hundreds of miles away ... That didn't make him any less a "lost child," as in the story about the bears: he entered an empty house, he wondered who lived there, with a feeling of imminence ... at any moment the owners might interrupt him ... It didn't matter that it was his house, that he'd lived there all his life; this was a detail that had no decisive weight to the overall meaning of the story ...

We were a pair of healthy, normal children, nice enough to look at, good students ... We adored our mothers and venerated our fathers, and feared them a little as well; they were so strict, such perfectionists ... I believe we were the quintessence of petit bourgeois normalcy. And even so, though we didn't realize it, it all rested on fear, the way the rock floats on the crest of the lava at the end of *Journey to the Center of the Earth*; fear—it might be said, the lava—was the biology, the plasma. To simplify by putting things in successive order, first came the fear the pregnant women felt (that is, it was beginning before we began ourselves), fear of giving birth to a monster. Reality, aristocratic and indifferent, followed its course. Then the fear was transformed . . . It's all a question of the transformation of fears: this makes society volatile, changeable, worlds change, the distinct successive worlds that, added together, are life. One of the avatars of fear is: that the child is lost, that he disappears . . . Sometimes the fear is transferred from the mother to the father; sometimes it is not; the child registers these oscillations and is transformed in turn. That it might be the parents who disappear, that the wind might fall in love with the mother, that a monster might pursue them, that a truck driver might never lose his way because he carried his house with him like Raymond Roussel, etc. etc. etc., all that, and much more still to be seen, is part of literature.

Now I remember a type of candy that the children of Pringles adored in those days, a kind of ancestor of what afterwards became gum. It was very local, I don't know who invented it nor when it disappeared, I only know that today it does not exist. It was a little ball wrapped in parchment paper, accompanied by a little loose stick, all very homemade. One had to chew it until it got spongy and grew enormously in volume; we knew it was ready when it no longer fit in our mouths. We'd take it out, and it would have transformed into an extremely light mass that had the property of changing shape when blown by the wind, to which we exposed it by putting it on the end of the little stick.

That must be why it was only a local candy: the winds of Pringles are like knives. It was like having a portable cloud, and seeing it change and suggest all kinds of things ... It was healthy and entertaining ... The wind, which left us as we were (it limited itself to mussing our hair) ceaselessly transfigured the mass ... and there was no point falling in love with a particular shape because it would already be another, then another ... until suddenly it would solidify, or crystallize, into any one of the shapes that had been delighting us for so many minutes, and then we would eat it like a lollipop.

I said before, I think, that when it snowed at night Chiquito would come by at dawn and leave me, as a present for when I left for school, a snowman in the doorway of my house. For me, as for Omar, both of us ignorant of his secret life, Chiquito was a hero, with his truck as big as a mountain and his journeys across all of marvelous Argentina ... The neighbors praised his heart, his slightly childish gesture—which did more justice to his name than to his herculean physique—for building a snowman at those impossible hours when he always set out, just to give me a fleeting surprise, a little pleasure. Sometimes, when I went out on those occasions, the wind had already started to blow, and my snowman received me with eight arms, or a humpback, or more often with a Picassoesque twist, the nose at the nape of the neck, the navel on the back, both shoulders on the same side ... On my return at noon nothing would be left: it always melted.

But there was one snowman, (two or three winters before the summer in which the action of this novel takes place) that didn't melt. When I came outside I was taken aback. No one had told me it had snowed. It was still dark, but I could see well enough; in front of me there was a snowman, three and a half feet high, that originally, when Chiquito stopped by to make it before he left, would have been one of those friendly squat dwarfs that snowmen always are. But in the meantime the snow had stopped falling, the wind had begun to blow, and the snowman had been modified on all four sides. This didn't frighten me; on the contrary, I was so delighted I burst out laughing ... The fact that the snowman would melt within a few hours didn't worry me either ... but it did worry him.

"When the sun comes out," he said, "and it won't be long, I will turn to water and the earth will swallow me."

"When someone puts their foot in it they often say 'May the earth swallow me up,'" I said. Even as a boy I was very pedantic and a know-it-all.

"But I'm not saying that! I don't want to die."

I said nothing. I couldn't help him, but then to my surprise the wind spoke:

"That can be arranged."

The Snowman: "How?"

"You will have to accept my terms."

"And I'm not going to die?"

"Never."

"Then I accept, whatever it is!"

There I intervened, unable to stay at the fringes of any conversation:

"Be careful, this looks like one of those soul-selling deals the devil does, for example in ..." I started telling them, with a wealth of detail, the plot of *The Man Who Sold His Shadow,* which I'd already read (as an eight-year-old! How insufferable I must have been!). But the snowman interrupted me:

"And if I don't have a soul, snotface?" And to the wind: "What are the conditions?"

"Only one: that you let me carry you to Patagonia, where the sun does not melt the snow, and you let yourself be molded forever, every instant, by the winds. You will live forever, but you will never have the same shape twice."

"What a deal! Since you've already changed my shape anyway..."

"But listen, there we blow a thousand times harder than here."

"Don't exaggerate. What do I care, anyway? It's a deal, let's go."

I had nothing to say (and they wouldn't have paid me any attention anyway) since the whole business seemed pretty reasonable to me ... But didn't it always seem reasonable in these cases? Wasn't that the devil's best trick? Except in this case, since it was a snowman, it really did seem reasonable, no hidden trap. And yet ...

I watched as the wind lifted the snowman with a whirling "Ups-a-daisy!" and carried him away through the gray light of dawn.

24

I NEVER KNEW what I did that lost afternoon ...

In loss everything comes together. Loss is all-devouring. A person can lose an umbrella, a piece of paper, a diamond, a bit of lint ... It's all metabolized. To lose is to forget things in cafés. Forgetting is like a great alchemy free of secrets, limpid, transforming everything into the present. In the end it makes our lives into this visible and tangible thing we hold in our hands, with no folds left hidden in the past. I seek it, to oblivion, in the insanity of art. I pursue forgetting as well-earned pay for my fatigue and my memories ... What good is working? I'd rather be finished already. One more effort ... I would like all the scattered elements of the fable to come together at the end in one supreme moment. Except maybe I don't have to work to pull it off, in which case my efforts would be unnecessary. Or at least ... I should have thought it through better ... Instead of sitting down to write ... about the seamstress and the wind ... with that idea of adventure, of successiveness ... I'm not saying, Renounce the successiveness that makes the adventure ... but rather to imagine beforehand all the successive events, until I had the whole novel in my head, and only then ... or not even then ... The whole project like a single point, the Aleph, the monad totally unfolded but as a point, an instant ... My life set in the present with everything that has happened in it, which isn't much, which is hardly anything. Wasting time in cafés. I never found out what I did that lost afternoon ...

En fin. Now that I'm here, let's finish.

I'd left Delia in the twilight, lost and waiting. The wind came back with a small, perfectly gray thing.

"I didn't find the dress or the sewing kit. I'm sorry. I don't know what you wanted them for anyway."

"And this?"

"It's the only thing I found. Is it yours?"

"Yes ... It was mine ..."

It was her silver thimble, a precious souvenir, in whose little hollow Delia thought her whole life might fit, her whole life since she was born. And now that it looked like her life was coming to an end, or that it was slipping into an unintelligible abyss, she saw it had been worth the trouble to live it, there in Pringles.

"It's not just a common thimble," said the wind. "I've transmuted it into a Patagonian Thimble. You'll be able to pull anything you want out of it, whatever your desire tells you, whatever size it might be. All you'll have to do is rub it until it shines every time you ask for something, and I'll take care of that, I'm very good at rubbing."

Delia was about to answer him, because she'd finally found a good response, when she heard a distant sound and looked up.

There were people coming, from all four sides. Miniatures. Distant things have been made small. The function of truly large places, and Patagonia is the largest of them all, is to allow things to become truly small. They were toys. Four of them, and they came from the four cardinal directions, in a perfect cross whose center was Delia. Chiquito's truck, the Paleomobile, the Monster, and the Snowman arm in arm with the empty Wedding Dress. These last two came with little measured steps, like a bride and groom bound for the altar. But the speed of all four was the same, and it was obvious that in the end there would be a collision on the spot where Delia stood. She tried taking a step to the side, and the four right angles moved with her. The encounter would be simultaneous. (I could never have thought of such an appropriate image of the instant as catastrophe.) There was nothing to do. She closed her eyes.

But even simultaneity has an internal hierarchy: it's a law of thought. In this case, the principal thing, the irremediable problem, was that the Monster had found her. In the face of this circumstance it was pointless to close her eyes, so she looked at it.

It really was horrible. Like an abstract painting, a Kandinsky. And it was shrieking:

"I'm going to kill you! Carrion! Wretch!"

"No! No!"

"Yes! I'm going to kill you!"

"Aaaah!"

"Aaaaaaah!"

Delia fell to her knees. From that position she raised her eyes for the second time. The Monster was coming toward her. If motives for fear have already been given in the course of this adventure, this one trumped and transcended them all. She would have run away ... but there was nowhere to go. She was in Patagonia, limitless Patagonia, and she had nowhere to go—not the smallest of the paradoxes of the moment.

"Don't kill me!" she cried.

"Shut up, you whore!"

"I'm not that! That thing you said! I'm a seamstress!"

"Shut up! Don't make me laugh! Grrragh!"

It had grown a lot. Only a few feet separated them ... And then the wind came between them, as a last defense. He blew furiously, but the Monster only laughed harder. How little the wind could do against a transformation! The wind is wind, and nothing more. How could it have fallen in love with Delia? How could she have believed it? No one could be so innocent. The gentleman Sir Ventarrón, the wandering knight. He madly tried to slow the monster down, but he was nothing but air ...

An instant, too, has its eternity. We'll leave Delia in that eternity while I look after the other guests.

Chiquito and Ramón stopped their vehicles at a certain distance and studied each other for a moment. The former had Silvia Balero at his side, unhinged and dazed as a zombie. Only Ramón's eyes were visible through the narrow half-moon over the horn at the front of the rolling armadillo. At last the truck driver opened his door and stuck out a leg ... Ramón's eyes disappeared from the slot, and a moment later he was getting out through the back of his vehicle. They approached without taking their eyes off each other.

"Good afternoon," said Chiquito. "I have to ask you a favor, if you're going to Pringles; take this young lady with you. She had an accident, and it's hard to find transportation from here."

"And you?"

"I'm going to keep going south. I'm going to pick up a shipment, they've been waiting for me since this afternoon in Esquel. I'm already late."

"But then you're coming back, and surely you'll have room for her."

"The thing is, the lady urgently needs to be in Pringles. Tomorrow at ten she gets married."

"Married?"

"That's what she told me. You can imagine her state. She's hysterical. I can't stand her anymore."

"We've all got problems."

"True. Me too."

"But taking on other people's problems . . ."

"Listen, Siffoni, I found her there, all I did was open the door for her, I couldn't leave her in the middle of nowhere like that."

"Don't lie!" roared Ramón, and he pulled the mask out of his shirt pocket for the other to see. "You won her playing poker. You won her from me."

Chiquito sighed. He'd actually been aware of this, but he'd given it a shot anyway. They were silent for a moment. Ramón, calmer, suggested:

"You can just leave her on the side of the road. Someone will come by."

"Yes, I *can*. But she could make a lot of trouble for me. There's the matter of her wedding. Couldn't you do me a favor?"

"You know me, Larralde. I don't do favors for anybody."

This phrase was a password; it meant they had reached an agreement, without any need to go into details. The cards would decide. Not the matter of Silvia Balero, either; that was just an excuse. It was the other matter.

The wind, impartial, brought everything they needed from beyond the horizon: a table, two chairs, a green tablecloth, fifty-two cards and a hundred red mother-of-pearl chips. They sat down. The table was too big and they looked tiny across it, their eyes half-closed, like two Chinese. The wind shuffled and dealt.

PARIS, JULY 5, 1991